MUTE

Colin Neenan

Also by Colin Neenan

In Your Dreams

Live a Little

Idiot!

Thick

MUTE

COLIN NEENAN

To book Colin Neenan for a speaking engagement or his *What's the Story* school writing program, visit colinneenan.com.

For more information about *Mute* and other books from Edge of the World Books, visit edgeoftheworldbooks.com.

FIRST EDITION

ISBN 978-0-615-60843-3

Acknowledgements

First, I would like to thank my daughters, Alix and Cadence. They have changed the way I understand the world and have been more instrumental than anyone in making me the person who would write this book. You are the two best teachers I know-- I've learned more from the two of you than I will from anyone ever. I would also like to thank my fiancé, Penelope Koechl, who knows "story" like no one I've ever met and who has been consistently and profoundly supportive. I would like to thank Jennifer Pacelli for the amazing cover, my daughter Cadence for modeling, my sister Candice Neenan, my sister-in-law Nancy Neenan and Dayna Gerring for their kind and generous notes, German for his gentle but important thoughts, and his teacher, Mrs. Lavorgna-Lye, for her generosity in letting me work with her classes. Every one of her ELL students has a great story to tell, and I hope they can all find their voices here in America.

for

Alix and Cadence

GLOSSARY

falil: means 'permanent sin.' When a person causes another human being permanent harm, that is *falil*— permanent sin. A permanent sin can never be washed away. It cannot be forgiven until death. At death, a person's *falil* can only be forgiven if that person has made amends.

jalil: means 'hardship of life.' For generations, Pax's people have been poor and oppressed. They currently live under military rule. Soldiers are corrupt and can take whatever they want. Reading and writing are discouraged. People expect life to be difficult.

mojean: means 'best human.' Many believe this goodness comes from God. Many others believe this goodness comes from human beings making an effort to do the right thing. While life is always difficult, *mojean* is what makes life worth living.

Mordean: a character similar to Death in America and other societies. We imagine Death as a scary looking figure. Pax's people do not have any images of Mordean because Mordean cannot be seen or heard but only smelled. When someone is dying, they will smell Mordean. Sometimes the smell is sweet like flowers, and other times the smell is like a body that has already been dead for some time. If a person smells Mordean, their death will be within hours or days.

enwaa: means 'not ready.' It refers to women who are not ready to have sexual relations. Pax's people have a clearly defined understanding of when a woman is no longer *enwaa*. Almost all young women are *enwaa* well into their late teens and some into their twenties. Having sexual relations with a young woman who is *enwaa* is *falil.*

PART ONE

PAX

ONE

I could have saved her.

That is what I remember, over and over. It is what I think about. All I had to do was open my mouth. All I had to do was say no, I was not getting out of the car.

But I kept quiet. I let Maal curse at me in our language, and then I let Anna talk me into getting out of the car. I had seen her stumble, I had heard her laugh too loud. I knew she was drunk. And I knew Maal, knew what he would do, given the chance.

I could have stopped it from happening.

But I kept my mouth shut.

I wake up in the middle of the night and remember that night, standing in the cold, watching the red tail lights disappear. I lie here with my eyes closed, just wanting to get back to sleep, but I see blackness that goes on without end. I hope Poppy, my grandfather, is right. I hope there is no God. Not because I am afraid He will punish me. I am not afraid of what God will do to me because I know I deserve it. What I am afraid of is heaven. I am afraid Poppy is there and knows what happened. And I am sick when I think my dead mother saw it all.

I used to worry about the sins I might commit. It did not occur to me that my one *falil*[1] would be something I did not do.

---

[1] For an explanation of this and other words in Pax's language, please see the glossary just after the title page.

TWO

It is not bad here, in the detention center. The food is soggy and all smells the same, but there is plenty of it. The tall man in the suit said the guards would treat me like a human being, and they do. He also said I would have my own room, and I do. The tall man in the suit said he wanted me to have privacy, but I know that is not the reason I have my own room.

I met the tall man in the suit yesterday morning. They took me to a small bare room with a table and four chairs. The tall man shook my hand very quickly, like he couldn't wait to let go, and introduced himself in a voice that was so fast the words ran together.

With him was a tired looking woman with skin the color of the pale mud back in my village. She did not smile, and I thought she did not like me, but I was glad she was there because the tall man in the suit said she spoke my language. Very few people in America speak my language. The tired looking woman shook my hand and looked at me and pronounced her name slowly.

"Mrs. LaVenya."

The three of us sat down at the table. The tall man in the suit sat across from me and leaned forward, his elbows all over the table.

"Detective Patterson tells me you understand English," he said, smiling with his teeth. "Is that right?"

I hesitated. "*A little*," I said, in my own language.

"A little," Mrs. LaVenya said, in English.

The tall man in the suit nodded. "But you don't *speak* English, is that right?"

I nodded.

The tall man wrinkled his forehead. "How

did you learn English?"

"*Poppy, my grandfather, took me every week to hear the priest,*" I said, in my language. Mrs. LaVenya translated and I went on. "*Poppy would make me stay afterwards by myself while the priest taught catechism.*"

The tall man grinned, seemed to like this answer a lot. "You're Catholic, then?"

I shook my head. "*Poppy very much wanted me to learn English.*"

Mrs. LaVenya smiled and told the tall man what I said. He looked confused.

"But your grandfather did not want you to be Catholic?"

I was not sure what to say. "*The priest would not let Poppy come to catechism class because Poppy did not believe in God,*" I said, and let Mrs. LaVenya translate. "*I did not think the priest was mojean.*"

Mrs. Lenya had some trouble explaining to the tall man what *mojean* meant.

"It literally means *best human,*" she told him. "It is about how humans are good enough to help each other."

The tall man in the suit glanced at me, his lips pressed together. He liked it better when he thought I was Catholic.

"If you understand English, why don't you speak it?"

I said nothing.

"It's a common phenomenon with English language learners," Mrs. LaVenya said. "They call it the mute phase of language acquisition."

The tall man refused to look at either one of us. He scratched the back of his neck, like we were stupider than he had thought. "Give him the tape recorder."

Mrs. LaVenya just looked at me, and then she opened her large green purse and took out a device that was about twice as large as a cell phone. "*Have you ever used a recorder of sound?"* she asked, holding up the device in her palm. *"We would like you to tell us everything you know."* She showed me which buttons on the machine to push to make it work. Then she handed the recorder to me. I looked at it, there in my hand.

"What do I say?" I asked.

Mrs. LaVenya smiled again. *"Tell your story,"* she said.

My eyes jumped to her eyes, my heart leaping, my mouth falling open. *"You want me to tell my story?"*

"What's wrong?" the tall man in the suit asked.

"I don't know," Mrs. LaVenya said, watching me. *"Pax, is there a problem?"*

It took me a long time to find words, and when I did, I could only whisper them. *"My mother was right,"* I said.

"About what, Pax?"

Again I looked at the recorder. *"She had a vision."*

The tall man leaned back across the table. "Don't worry," he said. "Everything will be fine."

This I knew was not true. Everything would never be fine. That was the nature of *jalil*.

He looked at Mrs. LaVenya. "You need to convince him there's nothing to be afraid of."

Mrs. LaVenya did not say anything.

"Tell him!" the man said, his voice suddenly sharp.

Mrs. LaVenya glared at him, her mouth small. Then she turned to me and spoke in my language. *"I am supposed to tell you there is nothing to be afraid of."*

I looked down at the table top. I wanted to look across at the tall man. I wanted to tell him to go to hell. But instead I looked down at the table and did not move my eyes.

Mrs. LaVenya's voice changed, became soft. "*You know he's lying*," she said, in my language.

I nodded. I knew the tall man in the suit was lying. I also knew it was not me Mrs. LaVenya did not like.

It was the tall man in the suit.

THREE

My mother died so long ago I have to stretch my mind as far as I can to remember her. Sometimes I think I may not have my own memories of her at all. It may be that Poppy talked to me about her so much that he gave me my memories back.

It is hard for me to know what in my mind, if anything, belongs to me and what in my mind belongs to Poppy.

When I was a small boy, I remember sitting at the window looking out at the ocean, watching as Poppy steered his row boat to land. We did not have windows in our hut—just holes in the wall—and while I was sitting, a small bug landed on the windowsill in front of me. It looked like a grasshopper but was lighter green and had wings so thin I could see through them. I had never seen anything quite like it, and I took a pointy knife and pinned one of the delicate wings against the window sill. I was fascinated to see the bug squirm, its feet slipping as it tried to get away. When Poppy carried the fish up to the hut and saw what I was doing, he was so furious that for hours he could not even speak to me. When he finally did, there was a coldness in his voice that made my stomach feel empty.

"Perhaps tomorrow I should hold you down with a needle through your arm," he said, and did not console me when I burst into tears, thinking about a needle going into my flesh and straight through my bone.

When I had run out of tears, Poppy wrapped his arms around me and told me that each and every creature—from bugs on the windowsill to the fishes we eat to the people we love—deserved our *mojean*. He said that many people believed that *falil* could only be committed against people, but that he had battled with many fish who had more heart and deserved more respect that many humans he knew.

"The priest," I argued, remembering my catechism, "said that only humans have souls, so we are the only creatures God really cares about."

Poppy blew air through his lips. "The priest does not know what he is talking about."

"Poppy, why do you make me go and listen to the priest every week if he does not know what he is talking about?"

I was never allowed to miss either the service or the catechism.

"Do you want to go to America," Poppy asked, "and not understand English?"

The other children in my village who went to listen to the priest did so because their mothers or their fathers believed in the priest's God. Poppy made me go listen to the priest because he wanted me to learn English.

"Do you want to arrive in America and have no idea what people are saying to you?"

"Poppy, we are the poorest people in our village. How am I ever going to get to America?"

I did not understand why we were so poor. Poppy was known for being the hardest working fisherman in the village, going out earlier than anyone else and almost always catching more fish. But we never had sugar for our coffee, like many people did, and Poppy went drinking only once a month while all the other men of the village went every week or more.

"With no money for sugar," I said, "how could we afford even the bus fare to the airport?"

"Pax." Poppy stared into me. "Have you stopped believing your mother?"

I bowed my head. According to Poppy, the last vision my mother had before she died was that I would go to America.

He walked over to our washing basin and took from the top shelf the one book we owned. It was in English. According the priest, it was called *Gulliver's Travels*. "What did your mother want?" Poppy asked, holding up the book.

"Poppy—"

"What was her dying wish?" he asked.

"She wanted me to learn how to read and write," I said.

"And why is that?"

"Poppy—" I was embarrassed. Every time we went over my mother's last vision before she died, I was embarrassed. But Poppy was not about to let me go without saying it.

"What did your dying mother see?" he asked.

"Poppy, this is silly," I said.

He shook *Gulliver's Travels* at me. "What was your dying mother's vision?"

I sighed, defeated. I did not believe this

would ever happen, but Poppy had faith in visions. I bowed my head. "That I would go to America and tell my story."

FOUR

The next day Mrs. LaVenya came back by herself, carrying two large cups of coffee. She did not know what I liked, so she made mine the way she liked hers.

"Lots of cream and sugar," she said, speaking English.

I pulled off the top of the cup and looked at the light brown liquid. Poppy and I almost never had sugar for our coffee. I had never had it with cream.

I took a sip. It was very delicious. But it did not taste like coffee.

Mrs. LaVenya said the name of the tall man in the suit so I could understand it—Roger Salinger. She told me he was a lawyer whose job it was to get Maal in jail.

We were back in the bare room, sitting across

from each other at the table. I proudly reached over and gave Mrs. LaVenya the tape recorder. I sat there sipping my coffee that did not taste like coffee while she used headphones to listen to what I had recorded. I waited for her to hear the last line I had spoken so she would understand why I had been so shocked when she said to *tell my story.*

She smiled, turned off the recorder, and pulled off the headphones.

"*Do you remember your mother?*" she asked, in my language.

"*Sometimes I think I do.*"

Mrs. LaVenya nodded and then sighed. "My father died when I was four," she said, in English, her eyes looking far away. "When I was seven my mother married a man who was not a good man."

I did not know what to say. The day before I had thought Mrs. LaVenya looked tired. Now I wondered about the difference between tired and sad. Were there people in America who understood *jalil?*

After a few moments Mrs. LaVenya shook herself, like she had dozed off. She smiled at me and again spoke in my language. *"I guess we all have our own story."*

I wanted to ask Mrs. LaVenya to tell me her story, but I did not know if that would be considered impolite.

"Listen, Pax," she said, holding up the recorder. *"What you said into the recorder of sound is very good, but if you want to tell your whole story, you need to hurry."*

I squinted because I did not understand. *"Detective Patterson said it would be weeks before we went to trial."*

Mrs. LaVenya shook her head. *"You have two days."*

"DAYS?" My stomach tried to run far away

from me.

"*The trial starts Friday,*" Mrs. LaVenya said. "*They want to get your testimony as soon as possible.*"

I put my coffee down on the table.

Mrs. LaVenya looked at me for a long time before speaking. "*Has anyone told you what will happen after you testify at the trial?*" she asked, in my language.

I rubbed my fingers along the smooth surface of the table top. "*They will send me back to my country.*"

Mrs. LaVenya nodded. "*If you testify, they will send you back to your country.*" She held up a finger. "*And if you do not testify, they will send you back to your country.*"

"*I will testify,*" I said.

"*You can tell us that you have decided not to testify.*"

"*I will testify,*" I said again, watching my fingers slide along the smooth surface of the table top. I could feel Mrs. LaVenya watching me.

"*Maal's father has put a ransom on your head.*"

I did not speak, did not move my eyes from the table top.

"Maal's father has promised to pay a very large amount of money to anyone who kills you before you testify against his son."

Again, I did not speak, did not move, except to slide my fingers along the smooth surface.

"Pax, you do realize," Mrs. LaVenya said, leaning forward and speaking more softly, *"that you do not need to testify?"*

"Yes, I do."

"They will deport you back to your country whether you testify or not. It makes no difference."

"It makes all the difference," I said, *"when the falil is mine as well."*

"Falil? Yours?" Mrs. LaVenya shook her head, seemed confused. *"But Pax, you did nothing wrong. Anna said you tried to save her."*

"Anna does not know everything about me," I said,

and reached over and took the recorder.

FIVE

Back in my village, girls liked me. I know that sounds like bragging but it is not, because I know Poppy deserves all the credit.

He told me how to talk to girls.

"Men are dogs," he would say. "They love to howl, but they do not listen."

He told me that because girls are used to men being dogs, it is a great and wonderful surprise when one of us does not act like a dog.

"Ask a woman questions," Poppy advised me. "Be interested in who she is. Be interested in what she has to say. Treat her like a good friend."

This seemed too simple to me, too obvious, but I was wrong. Girls loved to talk to me—even Tera, the most beautiful girl in our village—because I would ask questions and was genuinely interested in what they had to say. Soon girls were coming to our hut to say hello. Poppy saw this and gave me more advice.

"Move slowly when you kiss a woman," he said. "If she moves away, do not follow. If her lips meet yours, listen to them. Let her lips, her tongue make the decisions."

Just a few days later, my heart beating like I had run through the village as fast as I could, I kissed Kal, who lived along the river. I moved so slowly that she leaned forward to meet me. I listened to her lips, like Poppy had said, and let her do everything first. Soon we were holding each other so tight that I had to stop and catch my breath.

"You look like you have broken your head," Poppy teased when I came home that night. "Can you remember your name?"

He let me sleep that night, but the next morning he came home earlier than usual from his morning fishing and made us an extra cup of coffee.

"Kal's father is worried," he said.

"We kissed," I insisted. "That was all."

"He is worried that Kal likes you."

"Does he not want her to like me?"

"How old is Kal?"

"She is my age," I said. "Sixteen."

"Is she a woman?" Poppy asked.

I was not sure what he was asking.

"Is she a woman or is she *enwaa*?"

My face felt hot. I was embarrassed, talking about this. "She is *enwaa*, of course, Poppy. I know that."

"And does your penis know that?"

"Poppy—"

"It is *falil* to have sexual relations with a girl who is *enwaa*."

"I know this!" I was almost shouting.

"Even if the girl wants to have sexual relations with you," he said. "If she is *enwaa*, it is a permanent sin to be with her."

"Kal does not want to have sexual relations with me, Poppy. No one wants to have sexual relations with me."

I thought it was silly, that we were having this conversation. All I had done was kiss a girl. I did not expect anything else would happen for a long time—years, most likely. But that night Kal and I met at the beach, and she had a large blanket with her. Soon we were on the blanket, holding each other tight and moving against each other. Then Kal reached for me through my pants, and I suddenly understood why Poppy had asked if I knew and if my penis knew. My penis knew nothing but what it wanted to know. When I grabbed Kal's hand and pulled it away, she was shocked. First she was shocked, then she held me tight like she never wanted to let go.

The next day she told her friends that she

was in love.

SIX

Soon everyone in the village knew that Kal had strong feelings for me. And my cousin Maal came to my hut to visit me.

Maal had been born eight days before I was, but we did not see much of each other. Maal was the richest boy in our village. His father had moved to America and sent money, and Maal and his mother lived in a two room house with windows made of glass and a roof that did not leak. Sometimes they took the bus to the city, and Maal would come back with candy that was more delicious than anything I had ever tasted.

Everyone wanted to be Maal's friend. I was jealous of Maal, but Poppy said both Maal and his mother were walking proof of the *jalil* of life.

"Money is nice," he would say, "but it does not make up for losing a baby daughter."

Maal and I were three when his mother gave birth to a daughter who had trouble breathing and died five months after her birth. Maal's mother was not seen for weeks afterwards. When she finally came out to face life again, people would say that her laugh died with her daughter.

Maal's laugh survived the death of his sister, but it was a mean laugh that usually included making fun of someone. Even though Maal was my only cousin, Poppy never encouraged me to play with him.

It was not until I was six that I understood why Poppy did not want me around my rich cousin. At the celebration of the sun, Maal managed to get all the five and six and seven years olds together, boys and girls, and told them I had a tail. Everyone began to laugh, and I could see the boys looking at me with eyes that were large with surprise and the girls looking at me with eyes that were squinting with disgust.

I made the mistake of pulling down my pants to prove it was not true, that I did not have a tail. Maal pointed to my bare behind and roared with laughter, claiming he could see the scar where Poppy had cut off my tail. I twisted my body around as far as I could, and even pulled my cheeks apart, to see what Maal was talking about. I started to cry, thinking it was true and wondering why Poppy had never told me. Maal convinced the boys and girls to run away from me because a boy who wanted to show off his bare behind could not be trusted.

I listened to Poppy after that and stayed as far away from Maal as I could. Even though he was popular because he was so rich, there were other children who stayed away from Maal, as well, because he was known for having a bad temper when he did not get what he wanted. Maal would scream at people, and was known to hit people, once even breaking the front tooth of a boy.

I was surprised and suspicious when he appeared at the hut. Poppy was out on his boat, fishing, so I was alone with Maal. I offered him coffee, but he refused because there was no sugar. Instead he sat down and asked me about Kal. What did I do? Why was she in love with me? What was the sex like?

He seemed relieved to find out that I was still a virgin, I think perhaps because he himself was still a virgin. Maal continued to ask about Kal, though, and I admitted that Poppy had more to do with Kal liking me than I did. I told him all the things Poppy told me about how to treat a woman. Maal nodded as he listened and went away.

Less than two weeks later there were rumors of Maal and Tera being seen together, and awhile after that Maal came by the hut a little after dawn, as Poppy and I were cleaning the morning catch of fish. It did not take long for Maal to announce that he was no longer a virgin, and he jokingly thanked Poppy for his advice.

"'Let her lips, her mouth make the decisions,'" he said, quoting what Poppy had told me and I had told Maal.

Poppy froze on the spot, then dropped the knife he was using to gut the fish and walked away without a word. He was gone all day, and when he came back home, after the sun had gone down, he was drunk.

"Tera has been crying all day and her mother does not know what to do," he said, standing with arms crossed in front of the lantern, his shadow towering behind him on the wall and roof of our hut. "If you ever again share what I tell you with someone who has a blind soul, I will haunt you when I die and make your penis shrivel to the size of a toothpick."

I shared nothing Poppy told me with Maal or anyone else ever again.

SEVEN

Last year, when Maal and I were eighteen, his father wrote and sent money, wanting Maal to come to America. We were all jealous, but I tried not to show it when I told Poppy. He had apparently already heard the exciting news because he simply continued to stare out at the ocean.

"Is it good news, a son who is willing to abandon his mother?"

I did not realize that *only* Maal had been sent for, that his mother would remain in the village. I was bothered by what Poppy thought and was relieved when I learned that Maal and his father had plans to send for Maal's mother in six months. I could not keep out the scolding tone in my voice when I told Poppy, but he just turned and looked at me.

"We shall see what will happen," he said,

softly. This is an expression with my people, to *see what will happen*. It means that life is never what we think it will be, and is almost always worse than we imagined. Did Poppy think harm would come to Maal's mother before the six months were over? I did not ask because I did not want to know.

The night before Maal was to leave on the bus to the airport, a few of us passed around a bottle and admired his passport and other papers. None of us could read them, but I knew my numbers and recognized Maal's birth date on his passport. There was a mistake, though—the passport said Maal was fifteen instead of eighteen. Because we were drunk and we were jealous, we tried to tease him about being fifteen. Maal explained that his father wanted him to go to school in America and learn English, but that if the school knew he was eighteen, he would not be able to attend.

When the bottle was finished and we were all

pissing together on the beach, the waves white in the darkness, Maal announced that his father had a girl friend in America and would not be sending for his mother.

The next day I woke up with a hangover and did not tell Poppy that he had been right to expect the worst.

EIGHT

Some people would like to know what will happen in the future, but I am not one of them.

The eleven months after Maal went to America were some of the best days of my life. In the fall I turned nineteen, and Poppy would take me drinking with him and the other men of the village. When we talked, he treated me like an adult. And even though I was half the fisherman Poppy was, there were mornings when he would let me take the boat out by myself.

I am grateful that I was too blind to see what was coming. It never occurred to me anything was wrong until Poppy went to bed without cooking dinner.

There is a saying in my country that a fisherman who enjoys eating fish must be a very good cook.

Poppy loved fish, and to him, cooking was like a religion. He once told the priest that a grilled piece of fresh fish with a nice glass of wine was the closest he'd ever get to heaven. The priest just smiled, too smart to take the bait.

All I could remember, my whole life, was eating Poppy's cooking. So when he went to bed without cooking, I knew he had to be very ill.

But when I found him awake, sitting up and drinking hard alcohol, I thought he had gone out of his mind. He only drank one Saturday night a month and rarely got drunk. This was Tuesday, and he was already slurring his words.

"Do you know who you are?" I asked, worried he had perhaps knocked his head with an oar.

"I am dying," he said. "*Mordean* is here."

"Poppy, no," I said. "You're drunk. You don't know what you are saying."

"Do not be sad," Poppy said. "To me he smells like salt on the skin after making love to a woman."

"Poppy, you're drunk."

"This is not going to be easy for either of us."

I pointed at the bottle, wanting to blame the alcohol. "We should talk when you are sober."

Poppy shook his head and smiled at me. "You should have a drink."

"Poppy, this is craziness," I shouted. "You don't believe in God. How can you believe in *Mordean*?"

"Because I have never smelled God," Poppy said. "Mordean fills my nose."

I shook my head. "Why are you giving up?"

"I have been in pain for some months," Poppy said. "My time is here."

It hurt to think of Poppy being in pain for so

long and not saying anything to me. He watched me and seemed to know what I was thinking.

"It is not a comfort to me for you to know my pain."

"We need to get you help."

"Pax," he said, gently. "Let us part friends."

"We need to get you to the hospital," I said, although I did not know how we could afford to do this. Could Poppy ride the bus? Did we have enough money for two tickets? Was there someone we could borrow from? My mind was racing ahead to think of who might have money that they would be willing to lend when Poppy cleared his throat and spoke up louder than before.

"You need to promise to do as I ask."

"What do you need?"

"I need you to go to America," he said.

I stared. Was he running a high fever? Had he lost his head?

"Your mother's greatest hope was that you would go to America and tell your story."

"But going to America is not something we will ever be able to afford."

Poppy tossed something toward the foot of his bed. It was a small burlap sack tied with a red thread. "Your mother and I have been saving since before you were born," he said. "Your mother made me promise to send you to America. This is why we never had sugar for our coffee. We were saving for you."

Poppy's feet stuck up long and boney under the thin blanket. I looked at the burlap sack sitting between them. "We can pay for an ambulance. We can get you to the hospital."

Poppy shook his head long before the words were out of my mouth.

"We can get you better."

"I'm not getting better! This is what you need

to understand. *Mordean* does not go away alone."

"We need to talk to the doctors. With enough money, they can do miracles."

"I will not spend your money to find out what I already know."

"I do not want the money. I do not want to leave. I like it here."

"You like not being able to read? You like not being able to write?"

"This is my home."

"Home is the people we love," Poppy said. "Soon you will be homeless."

"Poppy, stop."

"Listen, Pax." Poppy took a deep breath and spoke slowly. "Please respect the wishes of a dying man. I do not want you here when Mordean takes me with him. I promised your mother I would send you to America. I have arranged for you to live with Mal and his father."

"But Poppy, you know they are not mojean."

"But they are the only people we know in America."

"I want to stay here."

"You need to go tell your story. The only way I will be able to die in peace is to know you are already on your way."

This was too much. I turned and charged out of the hut but then stopped because I had no place to go. I wished I had taken the drink Poppy had suggested. I wished I had taken the bottle from him so he would stop saying such stupid drunken things.

Poppy called out to me from his bed. "Pray to your mother."

I stood up straight, as if Poppy had snuck up behind me and had jabbed my backbone with the point of a sharp knife.

NINE

It had been years since Poppy had told me to pray to my mother. When I was little and would cry because I thought Poppy had been unfair, he would tell me to pray to my mother so she could tell me who was right. As I got older and became aware that Poppy did not believe in God, I challenged him. How dare he tell me to pray to my mother when he did not believe in God? How could my mother still exist when God did not exist?

"I remember your mother," Poppy said. "I do not remember God."

I was not sure what to say to that, so I left it alone. "If God does not exist," I complained, "where did my mother go?"

"You are asking me?" he said, squinting. "Ask your mother."

I was horrified. How could Poppy talk like

this? To a boy whose voice had barely begun to change?

After that, Poppy stopped telling me I should pray to my mother. Now I was nineteen—a grown man—and I resented him for treating me again like a small child.

I went for a long walk along the beach, letting the waves pull the sand from under my feet. When I got home, Poppy was asleep. I took the bottle from him and drank what was left. I was not interested in sleeping and sat in the dark for a long time, listening to the waves. Eventually I dozed off, and my mother visited me in a dream. I do not want to talk about the dream except to say two things: I cried because she was so beautiful. And I did not doubt her the way I had doubted Poppy.

I woke up and knew I needed to go to America.

TEN

I had already missed that day's bus to the city and the airport, but I would be on the bus the next morning.

I wanted to spend my entire last day in the village with Poppy, but he sent me to almost everyone in the village, returning borrowed items and paying small debts. To Maal's mother I delivered a paper that said she had the right to live in our hut and use Poppy's boat. Before she became rich, Maal's mother had learned from her father how to fish—it had been many years since she had torn guts out of a slimy fish belly, but she was running out of the money she has earned from the sale of her two room house and needed to do something.

Mal's mother was saddened to hear Poppy was dying, and she was surprised to hear I was going to America to live with Mal. When I explained what the piece of paper said, that she could have our hut and our boat, Maal's mother looked at the paper and began to cry quiet tears.

"Please help my son," she said, wrapping her arms around me and pulling me close. "I know who he is. Please help him see *mojean*."

As I was leaving she gave me a photograph. It was a picture of her sitting with Maal and his baby sister in her lap, the two children smiling at each other. "Please give it to him. Show him there was a time of joy. Please tell him he was not always unhappy."

She became embarrassed when she realized how much she had said about her family and shooed me out of the house quickly. I ran back to our hut, ready to spend the rest of the day with Poppy.

He had my passport waiting for me. I did not apply for a passport, but with enough money, many things are possible in my country. Poppy had a lifetime of savings to spend.

Like with Maal's passport, mine said I was three years younger than I really was—young enough to go to school in America. In fact, the passport claimed I was Maal's twin brother. His father had agreed—for a fee— to take me in as his own son. I would go to school with Maal, and I would work nights and weekends in the restaurant. In six months I would be ready to get another job and move out on my own.

Poppy said he did not put a lot of trust in Maal's father, but that since he and Maal were the only people we knew in America, we had no choice.

Along with the passport, Poppy gave me all the papers I would need, including the ticket that would allow me to get on the plane. Finally he gave me a copy of my certificate of birth. The district building that kept records of births and deaths had burned down several years before, so the certificate

Poppy gave me was the original— on nineteen year old blue paper, very thin and worn. He was not sure I would ever need it, but he thought I should keep it well hidden because it might be handy at some point. I opened up *Gulliver's Travels,* which Poppy insisted I take with me, and slipped the folded piece of blue paper between pages 248 and 249. At page 310 and 311 I slipped in the photograph of Maal and his mother and sister.

The next day I woke up crying. Poppy cried, too, and congratulated us both on acting like women. He was convinced that women were better than men because they were not dogs, did not have penises to think with. Poppy believed men were better off when they were more like women, and he was proud of both of us for crying. Poppy was able to get out of bed and drape his arms around me, but he did not have the strength to hold me tight.

The bus ride was miserable. I could not eat

breakfast and now I was hungry, and I felt guilty for being hungry when Poppy was dying. I was mad at myself for going, and I was mad at my mother for coming to me in the dream and telling me to go. Why did I listen? Did it make sense to listen to a dead women, even if she was your mother?

At the airport were guards who looked at your papers to see if you could get on the plane. My hands shook as I handed over my passport. The guard was in a uniform that was too big for him, and he took a long time looking at the passport. Then his eyes looked up at me, and my heart pounded like it was trying to give me away.

"Sixteen, huh?" he said. "Seems like everyone going to America is sixteen."

On the plane I felt guilty for being excited. When the plane accelerated so fast down the runway, I thought the pilot was young and was panicking because he did not believe we would get off the ground. Then the runway stopped being so bumpy and we tilted way up toward the sky and I realized we were no longer on the runway.

We were flying.

We were headed into the sky, and I was silly enough to remember a fairy tale told in our country about a man who climbed a mountain so God could hear him better. We might have been closer to God, on the plane, but God was not going to hear us any better, that was for sure. The plane was so loud I worried again that something was wrong, but no one else looked at all concerned. I wondered what kind of person I was, leaving my dying grandfather behind and spending all my energy worrying about my own safety.

Aside from being loud, the plane was also very boring. I was not used to sitting in a chair, even a very comfortable one. I got out *Gulliver's Travels* and looked again at the blue paper of my certificate of birth. Then I began studying the illustrations in the book, including a drawing of a giant visiting little people and a little person visiting giants. For the first time I realized that the giant visiting the little people looked exactly like the little person visiting the giants. Were they both Gulliver? In his travels, did he visit a land where he was a giant and then another land where he was a little person?

I felt like a little person visiting giants, coming to America. I could even imagine what it would be like, having to run out of the way of the footsteps of the giants, just to stay alive.

I looked at all the illustrations in the book. Then, as I was closing it, something fell out.

A photograph of my mother.

A groan escaped me. It was so loud that, even with the sound of the airplane, the man sitting next to me looked over and asked if I was all right.

It was the only photograph of my mother

that we had. In it, her belly is huge because I am inside her. My father—*the coward*, Poppy called him— had left the village as soon as he found out my mother was pregnant, but in the photograph my mother is hugging her belly and she is smiling like she did not have a care in the world.

The photograph was Poppy's most prized possession. He should not have given it to me. Looking at it, I felt an emptiness in my stomach I had never felt before. I should not have left Poppy, should not have left him alone. I no longer trusted the dream my mother entered, no longer trusted my memories of who she was and what she told me when I was little. I realized that my memories were probably just what I imagined from the stories Poppy told me about her, over and over. The stories allowed Poppy to give me back my mother, even after she was gone.

But if my memories of my mother were not

real, was the dream she came to visit real? Had my mother really come to tell me to go to America?

Or I had I made the decision myself?

ELEVEN

Maal and his father met me at the airport. Maal was not as skinny as he had been in our village, and his father had a belly the size of three large fish. Maal's hair was cut short but stood up on end and looked shiny. The two of them walked on either side of me through the crowded airport that was big enough to be a city.

"*You're going to love it here,*" Maal said, in our language, handing me a cell phone.

I knew what it was right away because when the soldiers came to our village to look for criminals, some would have cell phones with them and sometimes they enjoyed showing them off.

"*Take a look,*" Maal said, grinning as he pointed to the cell phone. On the small screen I saw two naked women, kissing. I immediately looked away and tried to hand the phone back to him.

"*Why would you show me this in front of all these people?*"

"*It doesn't matter,*" Maal said. "*In America no one cares if you have a hardon.*"

"*I care,*" I said, still trying to give him the phone.

"*It's your phone,*" Maal's father said. "*I will take the charges out of your pay.*"

Poppy had said to be ready for Maal's father to get as much of my money as he could.

Maal closed the phone, which folded in on itself. "*It's like having a whorehouse in your pocket.*"

I looked doubtfully at the small device that fit in the palm of my hand. I was not sure it was a good thing to have a whorehouse in my pocket. How would I be able to concentrate, knowing it was there?

"*You can have tits and ass all night long,*" Maal said. "*But be careful. Do not be getting a hardon for Anna.*"

I was not sure I should ask, but I needed to know. *"Who is Anna?"*

"My girlfriend," Maal said.

His father, on my other side, laughed loudly.

"She will be," Maal insisted.

"How do you know this?" his father asked. *"Has she asked you to touch her p---y?"*

I kept my eyes straight ahead, could not believe what I had just heard. In our village, a father would never use that word when talking to his son.

"She will," Maal told his father, angrily, and then turned to me. *"American girls are sluts."*

I did not look at either of them. I held the cell phone in my hand because I did not want to put it my pocket. I did not want a whorehouse in my pocket, did not want to know that I could see naked women any time I wanted. Were American girls really sluts, like Maal said? How was I going to learn English if girls offered me sex all the time?

TWELVE

More frightening to me than anything in America was the cold. The plane had been connected to the airport building, so I did not face the cold until we had walked all the way through the warm building and through doors that opened for us all by themselves. As soon as we came through the door an icy wind shoved me back and took my breath away. I knew, of course, that it got cold in New York, that it even snowed. But I had never experienced cold like this before and was surprised at how mean it felt, as if the wind would have been happy to see me turn into ice.

Maal laughed, looking at my reaction. When we got to the car, there was an old jacket of Maal's in the backseat. It had a hood with fake fur around the edges.

"It's ugly but warm as hell," Maal said.

It was not warm when I first put it on, but soon I was very glad to have it.

Almost as frightening as the cold was leaving the airport. We went on a road with three and then four lanes in both directions and then over a towering bridge that was big enough to reach over three villages. Maal's father drove incredibly fast but no faster than all the other cars.

The ride to Bridgetown went by quickly, and Maal's father found parking outside their apartment building. The apartment was on the third floor, and the stairs were steep and smelled like urine.

"Mrs. Murphy's cats," Maal's father explained. *"We're dealing with it, but cats take a long time to die."*

Maal and his father lived in a one room apartment that was three times the size of the hut I shared with Poppy. The apartment, though, was so filled with stuff that it felt crowded in a way that our simple hut did not. Poppy and I had two plates and two cups, but Maal and his father had many cups and plates and glasses, and they were scattered all over the table and in the sink.

On the stove were dirty pots with lids tipped up like crooked hats. There was a couch, a bed with another that pulled out from underneath it, two dressers, a large wooden cabinet, a short table, a padded chair big enough for two people, and an enormous large black television which Maal turned on as soon as we got there.

He flung himself on the couch facing the television and picked up a gray plastic box. On the television was a dark land where there had been a terrible fire that had burned everything. There were figures moving in the darkness, and Maal began pressing the plastic box. Explosions went off, and the figures started jumping up with bursts of red in their stomachs. Maal was shooting them, I realized, hearing groans now between the gunshots.

"S---," Maal said, staring madly at the screen. "F---."

His father showed me two empty drawers on the bottom of one of the dressers where I was to put my things. I knew I did not have enough to fill even one of the drawers, but I just thanked Maal's father, who said he would be back soon and left. I knelt by the dresser and slowly took things out of my sack and put them in the bottom drawer. When I pulled out *Gulliver's Travels,* I turned and looked at Maal, still playing his game.

"Your mother gave me a photograph of you and your sister," I said.

"Get rid of it," he said, not taking his eyes off the television.

I waited until he stopped shooting people. *"She is holding the two of you in her lap."*

Maal almost shouted. *"Shut up and get rid of it."*

I did not speak again, just hid *Gulliver's Travels*

under my other things in the drawer.

Maal's father came home with a paper bag and pulled out a bottle with golden brown liquid. All of the alcohol back home was clear, but this golden liquid caught the light and seemed quite beautiful as Maal's father poured some into a small glass. He quickly drank it down and refilled the glass and put the bottle in the cabinet over what I knew was the refrigerator.

"*Do not talk to anyone,*" he told me, in our language. "*Maybe you know a little English, but you want to keep your mouth shut. This is a war zone—people either want to steal your money or send you home. I knew someone from the restaurant who was arrested and sent home for tossing a wrapper out of his car. Throw garbage on the ground, and the police will arrest you. They will use any excuse to send you home.*"

He drank the second glass of liquor and swaggered over to the large wooden cabinet, his keys jingling as he stuffed one into the lock and turned. Inside the cabinet were guns—big and small, long and short. More guns than I had seen in my lifetime, even when the military came to visit our village to threaten us. Maal's father took out a large handgun and cocked it.

"*Don't take s--- from anyone.*" He pinched the material of his shirt and pulled it away from his chest. "*Because of certain people I know, I am untouchable. That makes you, as family, also untouchable. If someone tries to give you s---, tell your uncle, who has many friends.*" He pointed the gun at my head and smiled. "*Remember. Family looks out for each other.*"

THIRTEEN

On Thursday Mrs. LaVenya came to visit again. She was carrying large cups of coffee with cream and sugar, and she also had biscuits with eggs and ham. For a moment I felt like I was being spoiled. Then my stomach ran away from me when I remembered the next day I would be testifying. Thursday would be my last full day in America.

Mrs. LaVenya was pleased when she saw how many tapes I had filled up with my story. I promised I would finish by the next morning, and Mrs. LaVenya nodded and had nothing to say. For awhile we ate our biscuits in silence. Then, since it was almost the last time we would see each other, I felt braver than I would usually feel about asking questions.

"*The man your mother married,*" I said, in my language. "*Can I ask how he was a bad man?*"

We were again in the bare room with the table and four chairs. Mrs. LaVenya put her biscuit down on its wrapper and stared down into the table.

"*We can talk about other things,*" I said, watching her face.

"He was bad like Maal," Mrs. LaVenya said, in English, her voice like the priest when he read from his book. "He was like Maal but worse."

I bowed my head, did not want Mrs. LaVenya to think I was watching her. Poppy had taught me that sometimes people do not want to be reminded that there is someone there listening to what they are saying. I remained perfectly still.

"When I was a young woman I believed that because it had stopped years before, it was over. I believed I could forget what he had done to me and move on." Mrs. LaVenya picked up her coffee and took a sip, but she did not look like she was aware that she was sipping coffee. Her eyes looked like they were seeing something far away. "I fell in love, like anyone else," she said. "And I got married, like anyone else." She put her coffee cup back down and did not speak for a long time. "But I could not be a wife," she said, finally, almost whispering. "I could not find joy where a wife should find joy."

I did not move, did not blink. I thought of Anna. I wondered if she would be able to be a wife.

"*But I decided to stay MRS. LaVenya,*" she said, in my language, her voice normal again. She even smiled. "*Please do not say a word about this to anyone, because they all think I am still married. They laugh because I talk about my dog but never about my husband.*" She turned her head and stared at the wall. "*It is easier if everyone thinks I am unavailable.*"

"*I will say nothing.*"

Mrs. LaVenya nodded and looked at me. "*I know,*" she said, and smiled. "*You are mojean.*"

I looked away from her eyes. "*I have a favor to*

ask," I said, my heart pounding, *"but you cannot tell anyone."*

Mrs. LaVenya looked worried. *"What is it, Pax?"*

I swallowed. *"I need paper,"* I said.

Now she looked puzzled. *"Paper?"*

"Paper of different colors," I said. I really only needed one color, but I had practiced saying all the colors exactly the same. *"Red. Green. Blue. Yellow."*

Mrs. LaVenya smiled. *"Red, green, blue and yellow paper?"* she teased. *"That's your big secret?"*

I still could not manage to look at her. *"Please tell no one."*

Mrs. LaVenya stopped smiling. *"Not a soul, Pax."*

I was able to look back at her again. I realized the next day would be the last time I would see Mrs. LaVenya, and I was surprised at how much I would miss her.

"*Is there anything else you need?*" she asked.

Knowing it would be our last day, there was one more thing I wanted. "*If you bring coffee tomorrow,*" I said, "*could I please have mine without cream and sugar?*"

FOURTEEN

Maal and his father let me sleep in my first day in America. I was surprised when I woke up and they were both gone. The sun was well up in the sky, but I was still exhausted. It surprised me that I could be so tired when I had not done anything the day before but sit in a bus, an airplane, and a car. The room was very cold and for a long time I stayed on my soft mattress, under the covers, feeling like a bug still wrapped in its cocoon. The ceiling above was white and smooth and made me feel lifeless.

I felt sick to my stomach that I had left Poppy, and I was angry at my mother for coming to me in my dream. First I was angry at my mother, and then I was angry at myself for believing it was my mother talking. If there was no God, and when we died we were just dead, then the mother in my dream was just my imagination. I had made her up, and I had made up what she told me, and it was all my own fault for coming to America, where the ceilings were pure white and made me think of nothingness.

I got up. Poppy always told me that rich people and smart people could be lazy, but the rest of us needed to be sharks and keep moving.

I had nowhere to go, so I started cleaning. Even though it was one room, I realized quickly there was a lot more to clean in America than in our hut back home. There were so many smooth surfaces—the sink, the counter, the toilet, the windows, the floor. Maal and his father had enough clothes and food and bowls and spoons for an entire village, and they left everything everywhere. I put away as much as I could and neatly stacked the rest.

When I had done everything I could find to do, I looked at the television and wished I knew how to use it. The day before, Maal had wanted me to play the killing game with him, but I did not feel ready to shoot people. Then he turned on the television and I saw the bright green of an enormous soccer field. Then—as he changed channels, I saw bright splashes of color—faces, a cartoon of a bird, cars driving incredibly fast, people kissing, shooting, running as fast as they could, standing there talking to us.

I wanted to watch the television but did not know what buttons to push to bring it to life. I had nothing left to do. I walked over and sat down on the floor in front of the dresser and opened the bottom drawer, where I kept my things. I pulled *Gulliver's Travels* out of the drawer and looked at the photograph of my mother when she had me inside her. It filled me with sadness, to look at it, but I was surprised that I felt even more sadness, looking at the photograph of Maal's mother, sitting happily with her two children in her lap. Maal had insisted that I get rid of it, but I could not do it. I did not want him to find it, however, and be angry at me for keeping it, so I hid the photograph of the three of them in the narrow gap under the cabinet filled with guns.

I put the book away and closed the drawer and went to the bathroom to pee. Then I stood at the bathroom sink and looked at myself in the mirror and began to cry. I did not know yet why I was crying, the tears flowing, the snot flowing—I could not stop and had to hold onto the edge of the shiny white sink to keep my balance.

Maal came through the front door from school while I was still crying. I quickly closed the bathroom door because I did not want to try to explain why I was crying when I did not know. So I closed the door but did not know yet how to lock it. Maal opened the door but stood just outside, staring at me.

"I am sorry for what life becomes," he said. This is an expression in my language that meant one thing and only one thing.

The words entered my ears, and I had difficulty breathing. I swallowed hard and bowed my head. It was odd, but now that I knew why I was crying, the tears stopped. I could feel it in me. I felt it open a hole in my heart, and I knew it would never completely heal.

Poppy was dead.

FIFTEEN

He did not believe in God, but Poppy did believe we could know things before we are told. He claimed he was in his boat, out at sea, when he knew I was being born, and he rushed back to greet me, arriving in time to hear my first cry. He told me he woke in the night, his eyes refusing to shut, and climbed out of bed to hold my mother's hand as she quietly breathed her last breath.

I was not there for Poppy's death, but still I managed to feel my loss without being told. As Poppy liked to say, especially when he'd been drinking, the world did not need God to be full of miracles. All the time, things happen that we cannot explain—it might have been Poppy's greatest joy in life, to wonder about what we did not know. It was also the reason it was so important to him that I come to America and learn how to read and write.

He was convinced that reading and writing could lead to a better understanding of what we did not know. He wanted me to have the tools to reach deeper into miracles and the other mysteries of life.

SIXTEEN

When Maal's father got home, he was respectful of my sorrow.

"I am sorry for what life becomes," he said, in our language.

I nodded and bowed my head.

Maal's father opened up the cabinet over the refrigerator and took out the bottle of amber alcohol and sat it on the table. It was a tradition in my village to offer a man alcohol when he had lost a loved one.

"Shall we get drunk together?" Maal's father asked. A generous offer.

I kept my head bowed. *"Is there work tonight?"* I asked. *"At the restaurant."*

"With your uncle, there is always work," he bragged.

Soon we were at the restaurant, and I was in the back of the crowded kitchen, washing pots and pans and dishes. I had been cold since I came to America, so the steam and the hot water felt good.

Maal's English was good enough that he had become a waiter. Once when he came back into the kitchen with a tray of dishes to be cleaned, he watched me working and shook his head at me.

"Life is a long journey," he said. "Slow down."

I nodded but did not listen. Poppy always said that the harder you worked, the easier it was to forget *jalil*. Washing the dishes, scrubbing food baked onto the pots, spraying down the deep metal sink, I was trying to forget. I could not quite grasp that Poppy was dead. Poppy had been there my entire life, so it did not seem quite real that he was not in our hut, getting to bed early so he could be out on the boat before dawn. He had always been, since I could remember. It did not seem possible that I would never hear his voice again. His laugh.

I was trying to hear Poppy's laugh when Maal rushed to the back of the kitchen with nothing in his hands. Anna, the girl from school who Maal liked, had just called in a takeout order for her and her mother. She would be there in fifteen minutes, and Maal wanted me to take my break so I could see her. He pointed to where in the kitchen I could stand so that I would not be in anyone's way but could see the opening in the wall where people came to pick up their food to take away.

I did not want to take a break but could tell it was important to Maal, so I cleaned two more pots and wiped my hands on my apron and walked to where he said I should stand. I felt foolish, standing there and not doing anything. Of course, with nothing to distract me, Poppy would not leave me alone. I remembered the way he whistled, gutting fish, and the way he would look at me when I said something stupid. I remembered the way he walked with a slight limp because of a broken bone when he was a child, and the way he sat up straight in the boat, watching the horizon.

I was thinking so much about Poppy that I lost track of where I was. A voice—a girl's voice—pulled me back. I shot a look toward the hole in the wall where people came to pick up take out and saw Anna. It had to be Anna—she was small, had blond hair, and her breasts were pushing up out of her shirt. She was handing money to the girl at the cash register, and she was chatting and did not stop. She was too far away for me to hear what she was saying, but I could tell Anna spoke English with an accent.

Like a shark smelling blood, Maal appeared from nowhere and put his arm around her. Anna jumped, then laughed, then hugged him, pressing her breasts against him. I was surprised at this— no girl from my village would press her breasts against a boy unless they were going out. Had Anna become

Maal's girlfriend? He would be very happy, but I thought she looked young for him. I was wondering how old she was when another waiter, taller than Maal, appeared, and Anna gave him a hug, as well, pressing her breasts against him.

Now I did not know what to think. Was it true what Maal said, that American girls were sluts? Despite showing off her breasts and hugging boys with them, I did not think Anna was a slut. In fact, I felt quite sure she was *enwaa*—although it was possible she did not want to anyone to know she was *enwaa.*

That would explain why she showed off half of her breasts. That would explain why she hugged boys. Some boys from my village would love looking at breasts and hugging girls all day, but I felt uncomfortable admiring Anna's breasts, even from this far away. If she had not been *enwaa,* it would have been different, but I did not want to ogle Anna and went back to the pots and pans and dishes. When Maal came by later to ask what I thought, I only nodded because I could not tell him what I really thought. Maal would not want to hear that I was sure Anna was *enwaa*. He knew that a nineteen year old man should not flirt with a girl who was *enwaa*, so if I called Anna *enwaa*, Maal would not forgive me.

"What did you think of her tits?" he asked, unhappy with my lack of enthusiasm.

I kept busy on the pot I was scrubbing. *"Does she always show them off like that?"*

"Don't be such a grandmother. They are beautiful."

I kept my eyes on the pot I was scrubbing. *"How old is she?"*

"It does not matter how old she is," Maal said, anger in his voice. "Not in America."

I knew enough to not say anything, to not

even look up. Maal stood there and angrily flicked a fly away.

"In two months she'll be our age," he said, defiantly, speaking in our language.

I looked up, both surprised and relieved at this good news. *"She's eighteen?"* I asked.

"You asshole!" Maal looked over his shoulder to make sure no one was there, then turned back to me and growled in our language. *"We are sixteen. Remember?"*

"But we're not six—"

"Shut up!" Maal said, cutting me off. *"In this country, we are sixteen. This is something you cannot make a mistake about."*

"But Maal—"

He turned and walked away. I did not see Maal or his father the rest of the evening.

Not until I walked back to the apartment and knocked on the door.

SEVENTEEN

Maal pulled the door open half way and stood, blocking my way into the apartment. "You are a stupid s---," he said, grinning, alcohol on his breath.

The door was yanked open the rest of the way and Maal's father was standing there. "Welcome, my son!" he said, slurring his words and holding onto the doorknob for balance. "Come in, come in. Let me buy you a drink."

I said nothing. I had no idea what had happened, but I knew enough to keep my mouth shut. When he still lived in our village, Maal's father was known for hitting people when he was drunk, especially Maal's mother, who claimed she bruised easily.

Maal's father gestured to the table and kept speaking English. "Please, my son, come and drink with me."

The apartment was dark and reeked of alcohol. On the table was a lighted candle, two small glasses and a nearly empty bottle of the golden brown liquid. Also on the table was my copy of *Gulliver's Travels*. They had gone through my things. I did not know what they were looking for, but I was glad I had hidden the photograph of Maal's mother under the cabinet of guns. At least they could not be angry at me for not getting rid of it.

Maal's father sat down heavily in one of the chairs and pointed to the other. "Sit, my son," he said, reaching for the bottle and filling the two small glasses.

I sat down. Maal stood behind his father, still grinning as he watched me. Hearing his father call me *son* made me very nervous.

"To family," his father said, holding up his glass.

I held up the glass in front of me. *"I am too tired to drink, uncle. Maybe Maal would want this."*

Maal's father put his drink back down on the table without looking at me. He reached behind his back and pulled out a gun and sat it on the table next to his glass and spoke in our language. *"It is not right to turn down a drink from your father."*

My heart was beating hard now, and I could see my hand holding the glass trembling. I brought the glass to my lips and drank down the golden liquid, which scorched my throat. I struggled not to cough, which Maal's father might consider an insult to what he had served me.

He drank off what was in his glass in a single swig and refilled his glass, emptying the bottle. "Tell me, my son. How old are you?"

I looked up at Maal, did not understand what was going on.

"Son, look at me when I talk to you," Maal's

father said. The fake cheerfulness was gone from his voice. I looked at him, his jaw set tight. "How old are you?" he growled.

I swallowed before answering. *"My passport says I'm sixteen."*

Maal's father scratched under his chin. "And what do *you* say?"

I looked down at the table, knew what I needed to say. *"Sixteen."*

"Smart boy," Maal said.

"Do you understand," Maal's father began, speaking in our language again, *"that there are people out there who hate us for coming to America? Who are looking for any excuse to ship us back home?"*

I kept my eyes on the table and said nothing.

"Do you understand that we cannot give them anything they can use against us?"

I nodded, holding my breath.

"Then why, my son, would you bring this with you to

America?"

I watched Maal's father's hand as he reached over to *Gulliver's Travels* and slowly pulled out my blue certificate of birth. It could have been the alcohol, but I got a sick feeling in my stomach, seeing Maal's father hold the only official proof of who I was. I had to fight off the temptation to reach out and snatch the blue paper out of his hand.

"If someone had found this," he said, holding it up, *"and realized that you had a false passport, it would not have been good for any of us."*

"You dumb s---," Maal added, in English.

His father leaned close enough for me to smell the stale alcohol on his breath. "Do not f--- with me, my son," he said, glaring at me as he held the blue piece of paper over the candle. At first the old paper would not catch, but then the far edge of it burst into flame. Maal's father kept looking at me as he held the burning paper. I thought he was going to let the flame reach his fingers, but at the last second he reached over and stuffed the ashes and what was left of the paper into my empty glass. It was stupid of me, but I felt a little like he was getting rid of me, like he was stuffing *me* into the empty glass.

He grinned again as he picked up his glass and sat back and sipped at it. "You'll like being sixteen again. You can go find your own fifteen year old slut, like Maal found Anna, and you can do whatever you like with her."

My eyes shot down to the edge of the table in front of me. I was embarrassed to hear a father say these words in front of his son.

"In America it is better to be sixteen," Maal's father told me. "If Maal was nineteen, he would go to jail for f---ing that slut Anna. But since he is sixteen, he can f--- her as much as he wants."

EIGHTEEN

Maal was in a foul mood the next morning as we walked in the cold to school. He had taken so many days off that the school had called his father, who warned Maal that if he did not go to school, he would not be able to borrow the car over the weekend. There was a party that Friday that Maal very much wanted to go to, so he had no choice but to go to school, even though he looked badly hung-over.

The entrance to the school was a mob of people, some going inside, some standing around, and a few kissing like they were ready to have sexual relations. I took a deep breath, determined to be brave, but inside was more crowded and the volume of noise—people calling out, yelling at each other, metal locker doors being slammed—made me feel like a small bird wanting to get away.

Maal pointed to a door and disappeared into the crowd. I went through the door and into a room that was quieter but crowded with adults and students. Everyone knew where they were going. All I could do was stand until a woman sitting at a desk looked up and waved for me to come forward. The woman was old and had short hair, like a man, but she smiled when I slowly walked up to her desk.

"Can I help you?"

I could not believe how hard my heart was pounding. I handed her my passport.

"You are. . . Pax."

I nodded.

"Welcome to Bridgetown High, Pax."

She sounded like she meant it, and I tried to smile. The woman led me down a hall to another woman who was young and pretty and did not smile at all.

This woman brought me into a small office

and asked me questions—when did I arrive in America? How long would I be staying? I was very nervous and could feel sweat dripping from my arm pits. I followed Maal's advice and did not look at her. Even though I understood most everything she said, I looked at the floor and pretended the words meant nothing to me.

The young woman typed into her computer and shook her head, muttering under her breath. It was clear her life had been easier before she met me. I watched as her fingernails, unnaturally long and painted blood red, clicked against the keys. A machine began spitting out pieces of paper, which the woman gathered together.

She led me out into the hallway, which was much quieter and less crowded than when I came into the school with Maal. The woman with the strange fingernails had stopped trying to ask me questions, so I had a chance to look into classrooms as we walked by them. I must admit that the first thing I noticed was that Anna was not the only one who showed off her breasts. I wondered if this was something I would be able to get used to or if I would need to spend all my time looking down at my feet.

The woman with the fingernails stopped at a door and opened it. Inside was a small classroom with a circle of about twelve desks. Nine of the seats had students in them, and one of those students was Anna. Her hair was different, pulled back, and I did a pretty good job of not looking at her breasts, which seemed just as big as they had been the night before.

One of the students got up out of her chair. Only it was not a student. It was the teacher, a plump woman with curly black hair who seemed like she was genuinely happy to see me. Her name was Mrs. Franklin. I shook Mrs. Franklin's hand but did not say anything and refused to look at anything other than her hand shaking mine.

"That is Pax."

I looked past Mrs. Franklin at Anna, who had spoken. She had an accent that I did not recognize and that made her difficult to understand.

"Hi, Pax!" She waved. "Do you want you should sit here?" She pointed to an empty seat two seats away. I was so grateful to know someone that I almost nodded my head. Then I remembered that I was pretending I did not understand English.

I waved back but then saw the boy sitting to Anna's left, staring like he wanted to hurt me. On Anna's other side was another boy who was also staring at me with his arms crossed.

Mrs. Franklin led me to the empty seat Anna had pointed to, looking at me as she talked slowly about the class.

"How do you know Anna?" she asked, as I

sat down.

"He and Maal twins," Anna said.

"Oh, I see," Mrs. Franklin said, looking at me again. I was not sure, but it seemed like she was smiling less than she had been. I stared at the tiles on the floor, which were worn and dirty.

"I pick up chicken. Maal point him out," Anna said. "I say cute eyes. Maal no like."

Some people laughed and looked at me. I was glad no one knew that I could understand English. People looked at me but at least they did not expect me to respond.

Anna and Mrs. Franklin were the only people in the class who talked a lot. Occasionally someone else would say two or three words, but everyone seemed happy to listen to Anna and Mrs. Franklin, who were pretty funny together. I did not always get the joke, but I was happy to hear people laugh. I had not heard nice laughing since before Poppy told me he was dying.

Everyone began to put their notebooks away. Then a loud bell rang three times, and everyone began to stand up and head for the door. Before I could even get out of my chair, Anna came over.

"What you have next?" she asked, and took one of the sheets of paper the woman with the long fingernails had given me. "B-13," she said, looking at the sheet. "I in B-11. I walk you."

The hallways were scary again, crowded with people. A group of five girls exploded with laughter, one girl jabbing her finger toward another girl. She sounded angry, but everyone was smiling, which confused me. How would I be able to tell what people thought, if they could be angry and smile at the same time?

"It beginner class," Anna leaned into me to be heard over the noise in the hallway. "I talk more than beginner, should be in your brother class. But read and write?" Anna made a sound with her lips like a small motor. "I suck read and write." She pointed with her finger at the side of her head. "My mom pregnant, she drink vodka all day. She born me stupid."

I was surprised Anna was telling me this. She did not know me. People from my village did not trust strangers with any information about themselves or their families, but Anna seemed ready to tell me everything about herself. Is that what people did in America? Would they tell strangers about their lives?

"I think you nice person," Anna said, and reached out and held my arm for a moment, looking at me in a way that made me not want to look back at her. Sometimes there are girls who are *enwaa* but do not want to be *enwaa*. They want life to happen faster than it should, and that makes them dangerous.

"Anna, hold up!"

I recognized Maal's voice through the noisy hallway and pulled my arm away from Anna. Maal did not look at me as he came up and gave Anna a hug.

"Your brother nice," she said, grinning, swaying her body.

"What are you talking about?" Maal gave me a quick glare. "What did he do?"

"Well, he good looking like brother—" Anna paused and winked at Maal. "But he talk to me. He no talk to boobs."

Maal actually liked this answer and draped his arm over Anna's shoulder. "You love it when I look at your boobs."

Anna removed his arm from her shoulders. "I love how Pax look at me."

Maal did not say anything at first. Then he turned to me and spoke in our language. "*Look at her again and die."*

NINETEEN

There is an expression with my people that no one in this world needs to go look for mosquitoes or misery— eventually they will both find you.

I avoided talking to or even looking at Maal the rest of the day. At work I did not take a break and learned to wash pots more slowly so I did not run out of things to do.

The next day in class, Anna called out to me when I walked in. I gave a small wave without looking at her and went over and sat on the other side of the circle. The tiles on the floor were just as worn and just as dirty. Before class started, I could hear Anna's voice.

"Pax look mad at me," she said to someone. "Why he is mad at me?"

I spent the class looking at Mrs. Franklin's

shoes. They looked painful to wear, pointy in front with a tall thin wedge under her heel that kept the back of her foot up high.

When the three bells rang to end class, I got to the door as fast as I could and walked hard toward my next class. I was almost there when Anna caught up with me and hit me on the arm with the back of her hand.

"What I do to you?" she asked.

I did not stop, did not turn. I was at the door to my classroom when Anna stepped in front of me. "Are you—?" She pointed at me, then pointed at the frown she was making. "—mad at me?" she asked.

I tried to step around her, but Anna moved back in front of me. I shook my head, kept my eyes down.

"Why you no look at me?"

"Anna!"

I almost said s--- in my language. Instead I

just backed away from Anna. Maal stepped in front of me, facing Anna, his back to me.

"What the f--- is going on?"

"Why your brother no look at me?" Anna asked him.

I could see Maal's shoulders relax. He turned his body and looked at me. Anna's toenails, I noticed, were painted black.

"Why Pax he no talk to me?" she asked.

Maal laughed. "Because Pax he no *can* talk," he said. "Pax he mute."

"He what?"

"*Mute*," Maal said, patting me on the back, enjoying himself now. "Mutes can't talk because their mouths don't work. No talking, no kissing, no nothing. Pax his mouth no work. Pax he barely know how to *eat*."

I could feel Anna looking at me.

"So listen, sweetheart," Maal said, putting his

arm around her waist. "You hear about the big party at JD's on Friday?"

Anna nodded. "My mother said she no will drive me."

Maal held his hands up at his sides. "How about you come with me?"

"You have car?" Anna asked, sounding doubtful.

"Of course I have car," Maal said.

"You sixteen only. No license."

"My father let's me drive with my permit," Maal claimed, his voice getting tighter with hope that Anna might really go with him to the party. "What time do you want me to pick you up?"

"This car is safe?" Anna asked.

"Very safe," Maal said, giving Anna's waist an extra squeeze. "It has air bags, special brakes. Everything."

Anna looked up at Maal, thinking. "It has

back seat?" she asked, finally.

Maal's mouth dropped open, a grin growing on his face. "An amazing back seat," he said. "Big and comfortable."

"Good," Anna said. "Your brother Pax he come, too."

TWENTY

Maal ignored me the rest of the week.

I went to class late each day so I could sit where ever Anna was not sitting. On Friday, though, I came to class as the three bells rang to start class, and Anna was not there. Was she sick? I was happy. I felt bad for being happy that she was sick, but it meant she would not go to the party. Maal would be angry all weekend, and he would probably take it out on me, but that was better than Anna going to the party with him.

I sat down and thanked Poppy. I did not believe he came back from the dead to make Anna sick for the party, but maybe, if there was a God, Poppy said just the right thing to convince God that Anna should not go.

But then Anna came through the door of the classroom and smiled as she walked over and sat next to me in the circle.

"You cannot forever avoid me," she said.

I was happy to stare straight ahead and pretend I did not understand what she said.

"Do you dance?" she asked, watching me. "I think you and me dance."

I almost shook my head, almost said out loud, *no*. I wished Poppy was there to talk to her. I was not sure what he would say, but Poppy would make Anna understand that dancing with me was not possible. He would also make Anna understand that the most important thing she could do in her life was to stay away from Maal.

TWENTY ONE

I was sick in the soul when school ended, thinking about the party. Back at the apartment I watched television. I was able to mostly forget about Anna and Maal, and I realized watching television was a good way to avoid life.

Then Maal came home and wanted to play his killing game. I went over to the kitchen area and started to clean, but Maal got mad because I was being too loud. I went into the bathroom and closed the door and locked it and sat on the edge of the tub. Mrs. Franklin had given me a book with many colors that she called the alphabet. Inside were bright pictures of many things—an apple, an arm all by itself, and a funny looking, long-nosed animal that she called an aardvark. It took two days before I realized that, in English, the words for all of these things began with the same letter.

I wished I had brought a piece of paper with me to practice my letters, but instead I got up and went to the sink and breathed closely on the mirror. It made the mirror like a cloud, and with my finger I wrote the letter for apple and arm and aardvark. I already recognized other letters, as well, but I knew it would take me a *long* time to use them.

Maal pounded on the door. He wanted to take a shower. Of all the things in America, the shower was my favorite. Back home water was always too cold or sometimes too hot, but with a shower the knobs would let you get it to be at exactly the temperature you wanted. I felt like a king, standing under clean water that was just the temperature I wanted.

I thought I would take a shower, too, when Maal got out of the bathroom, but then I realized I should not risk it. I did not understand time on clocks but it had been dark outside for awhile now. I knew that if I was in the shower when Maal wanted to go to the party, he would have been happy to go without me. So while he was still in the bathroom, I washed up in the kitchen sink. I was dressed with my shoes on when he came out.

Maal got dressed and went back to his killing game. I turned on a light so I could look at my alphabet book, but Maal made me turn the light off so the only light came from the enormous television. With nothing to do in the dark apartment, I sat down on the other end of the couch and leaned my head back. I almost fell asleep. Then I realized that might have been exactly what Maal wanted. I stood up and went to the window and looked out at the abandoned street. I was not sure I had ever felt this alone.

Eventually Maal turned off the television and headed for the door without a word. I grabbed my jacket and followed him down the stairs and out to the car, where I got into the backseat like I did on the way home from the airport. I stared out my window as Maal drove, playing loud music. The streets did not look as ugly at night. In fact, the many lights made things look magical.

Maal pulled up in front a building and honked. Across the street were the bright pink and white lights of a donut shop. I could smell the sweetness, but even more powerful to me was the rich smell of coffee. I pulled air in slowly through my nose and imagined making coffee in our hut, waiting for Poppy to come back from the morning fishing.

Maal honked again, longer this time.

Anna came out of the door to her building and skipped down the steps. When she climbed into the front seat, she filled the car with a smell like flowers, only too many flowers. She looked very pretty, and her breasts looked even bigger than usual. I looked back out my window, angry at myself for looking at them.

"Who want to dance?" Anna called out. "Who want to party, party, party?"

Maal turned up the music even louder than before. A man started talk-singing, saying the same thing over and over.

Slap that bitch, I had to slap that bitch, no bitch get to say no.

Anna was talking in the front seat, looking at Maal and looking over her shoulder at me, but I could not hear her because of the man talk-singing.

The lights and loud music and people in front of the house made it easy to know where the party was. The rest of the street was dark and crowded with cars. We had to drive down a block before Maal could find a place to park the car. I did not move from the backseat, knowing Maal would want to go ahead by himself with Anna, but when Anna got out, she opened my door.

"Hurry up, lazy bones. Hurry up."

I still took my time, but when I was finally standing, Anna hooked her arm around mine, the side of her breast pressed against me. I leapt away, like her breast had burned my arm. Anna looked at me.

"You don't want to friend me?"

All I could do was stare.

Maal laughed. "He too stupid to be friends," he said, putting his arm around Anna, who kept looking at me like I had slapped her face. Maal pulled her away and headed down the dark street back toward the party. I followed, two boat lengths behind, my hands buried deep in my pants pockets, trying to stay warm in the cold. When we got to the house having the party, I stopped and stood by the street and watched Anna and Maal disappear inside. My plan was to stay outside to be sure I would see when Maal and Anna left the party, but as I stood there it got colder than I ever imagined it could be.

I would not be able to help anyone if I froze to death, so I walked toward the front door and the loud music. Inside it was crowded and the music was so loud it actually scared me, the thumping beat taking over my heart. I was glad for the heat, though, and didn't even mind my ears burning after getting so cold outside. I saw a dark corner on the other side of the room, past people dancing, where I would be able to watch the front door, and so I slowly slipped through the bodies. Everyone had a large red cup in their hands, and the smell of beer was everywhere. I would have enjoyed drinking beer.

I reached the corner. I could see the front door, but because it was dark and crowded I would need to pay constant attention. I would have liked to get a red cup, but I could not be distracted, could not let my mind wander. The truth was that I would have enjoyed drinking a lot of beer, would have enjoyed forgetting that I would never see Poppy again. Would have enjoyed forgetting these girls were *enwaa* and that I should not watch them dance. Being drunk and watching American girls dance would have been fun. I could not believe the way American girls danced, and even sober it was hard not to watch. I could imagine how much harder it would be after drinking beer. The good news was, even if I did get drunk and wanted to flirt with someone, I would not have words. I was glad I could not do something I would regret. I realized being mute made it more difficult to get in trouble.

People were leaving through the front door, but I had not been watching and was not sure who they were. Did Maal try to sneak back out? I resented having to pay so much attention to protect

Anna. I was not her father. Where was her father? Why was he not watching out for his daughter? Why was he not protecting her from the dogs?

I thought I would need to go back outside to make sure Anna and Maal had not left, but then I saw them. They both had red cups in their hands, and Anna kept drinking from hers as she pushed through the crowd toward where people were dancing. When she found enough space to move and started to dance, I had to pull my eyes away. She was not dancing like she was *enwaa*. Her body moved like a wave, like she was a woman, like she knew exactly who she was and exactly what she enjoyed. It was disturbing. Had I been wrong about Anna? Was she more experienced than I thought? More ready than I had imagined?

I glanced back at Anna and saw her take a drink from her cup. And I realized that I hadn't been wrong about who she was. She was not a woman. She was *enwaa*.

But she was drunk.

TWENTY TWO

Suddenly the room felt very hot—the first time I had felt too warm since coming to America. I pulled off my jacket, trying to think.

Not even a small fifteen year old girl could get that drunk that fast on beer. Had Maal given her something else? Something more?

I was not sure what to do, and the loud music made it more difficult to come up with a plan.

Watch them. That was one thing I would do. I would not take my eyes off them for the rest of the night. If they left, I would leave with them. If Maal tried to take Anna upstairs, I would follow. He would be very unhappy with me and might want to fight me. It was a fight I would be stupid to win. Maal's father would be furious if I hurt Maal and might even kick me out. If I fought Maal, I would need to let him win, but I could not let him hurt me too much or I would not be able to help Anna.

The pounding music ended. I took a deep breath and felt like a weight had been lifted from my back, but the relief only lasted a few seconds before more pounding music began. Anna was tipping her red cup high, finishing what was left, and Maal took her hand and led her through the crowd. I kept my head down and followed them through the crowd into a hallway that led back to the kitchen. The overhead light made the kitchen brighter than any-where else. Half of the kitchen had few people, but the other half was more crowded than anywhere else. On the floor was a large metal barrel that had a black hose people were using to fill the red cups. Maal took Anna's cup and pushed through the bodies to reach the barrel. While he did, I saw him take something from his back pocket and pour something into one of the red cups

No.

I shook my head. This was not going to happen.

I waited until Maal filled the two cups and pushed back through the crowd back to Anna. He handed her the red cup. She took a sip and wrinkled her nose, but then she took another sip. I was afraid I would lose heart if I waited, so I swallowed hard, pushing the fear down my throat, and walked up to Anna and took the cup out of her hand.

"*Hey!*" she protested, smiling, surprised, reaching for cup. "That mine! Go get own cup!"

I sipped from the cup, which smelled like beer but tasted like something I did not know. Without looking at Anna or Maal, I walked over to the sink and dumped out what was in the red cup.

"What *wrong* with you?" Anna asked, shocked but not angry as she walked over and took the empty cup out of my hand. "It just beer."

I shook my head.

Anna stared at me. "You just shake your head!"

I refused to look at her.

"I knew! I knew!" she called out, pointing at me. "You understand! You understand English!" She looked at Maal, very excited, proud of herself. "He understand English!"

I refused to look at Maal.

Anna shook the red cup at me. "What you talking, it not beer?" When I wouldn't answer, she looked at Maal. "What he mean? What he talking about?"

"Maybe he thinks you can't drink," Maal said. "Maybe he thinks you can't handle beer."

"No *handle?*" Anna's mouth dropped open. "You think I no drink beer? I drink beer before. I drink *vodka!*" Anna laughed, was shouting now, enjoying her own joke. "When I inside mommy, I drink vodka every day!" Anna waved an arm and stumbled, then looked down at the white inside of her empty cup. "You want you should save me?" she asked, looking at me, smiling. "You want you should be Prince Charm? You know Sleep Beauty? You know Prince Charm? You want you should wake me with kiss?"

I still refused to look at her. From the corner of my eye I saw Maal whisper to her.

"*LEAVE?*" Anna's mouth fell open again and she shook her head. "No *leave!* I drink beer. I dance Prince Charm." Anna grabbed my arm, just above my wrist. "Prince Charm, you want you should dance with me?"

I tried gently pulling my arm away, but Anna would not let go. I pulled away hard and stepped back. Anna squinted at me and lost her balance.

"You think I poison apple?" she asked, swinging her hip and pushing out her breasts as she smiled at me.

Maal moved forward and stepped in front of Anna. "We need to go."

TWENTY THREE

I waited by the front door while Maal and Anna found their coats. I was having a hard time swallowing down my fear, but I was trying my best not to show it. I did not know how much Maal would tell his father, and I hoped his father would not be so angry he would tell me to leave the apartment. I would not know what to do or where to go, and I worried about finding someplace warm enough to stay alive.

"Prince Charm!" Even with the music, I could hear Anna before I turned and saw her wave to me. "It me! Sleep Beauty! Give Sleep Beauty hug!"

I held up my hands, my palms facing Anna to stop her. Back in the kitchen she thought it was funny, but now she looked hurt. Maal pushed her past me and out the door. I waited a few seconds to let them get ahead of me, and then I pushed out into the cold. The air was thicker than it had been, a foggy glow around the street lights. I could see my breath like small clouds. Up ahead Maal and Anna walked arm in arm, and I could see their breath all around them.

"Hello, Prince Charm!" Anna called back to me, stumbling, Maal holding her up. "You want you should rescue me?"

Maal said something that made Anna laugh and then said something that made her hit his arm.

"I am *not*," she shouted.

"Shhh." Maal looked over his shoulder to see how far away I was, then leaned toward Anna and said something I could not hear. She giggled like a little girl.

It felt like a long walk to the car in the cold, misty air. The fog seemed to get thicker as we walked.

When they reached the car, Maal wrapped his arms around Anna and pressed her up against her door and began kissing her. At first her arms hung down at her sides, and then she patted Maal on the arms and turned her face away.

"Watch out," she said. "We shock Prince Charm. He never kiss like that."

Maal snorted. "Prince Charming too stupid to kiss like that."

With the lower half of his body Maal still had Anna pinned against the car. She squirmed to get away, and for some reason it reminded me of the bug whose wing I pinned with the point of a knife. I walked toward them slowly with my head bowed and stood right next to them, by the back door.

"It cold out here," Anna said.

"I could make you hot," Maal told her, and Anna pushed at him and finally broke free and opened her door. From behind her Maal reached down between her legs and made Anna cry out and jump. I saw her glance at me, but I pretended I did not see anything and opened my door and climbed into the backseat.

Inside the car I could still see my breath. I hugged myself with my arms and was happy when Maal started the engine. Soon there would be heat. Soon we would be home and I could sleep.

Maal blasted the music, even louder than before, and reached over to Anna. I was behind her seat and could not see where his hand went, what part of Anna he touched, but I could see her head and shoulders tighten, like she was bracing herself.

"You need drive," she called to him, over the music, pushing Maal's hand toward the steering wheel. "Go. Go."

I saw Maal's jaw flex like an arm muscle. He was not happy. It reminded me of when he was the rich little boy back in our village. When he did not get his way, he would hold up his fists, angry with the world.

Anna turned down the music.

"Please," she said, soothing him. She, too, could sense the anger. "Drive, please," Anna said, patting Maal's hand, which was still on the steering wheel.

I shut my eyes, bowed my head, and leaned against the door. I did not want Maal to know that I had heard or seen any of this. The car began to move, finally. I pretended to sleep. I felt exhausted, like I had been up all night, and sleep really almost came to me. I was in a place between being awake and asleep when the car came to a stop and the music on the radio was turned off.

"*Get out*," Maal said, in our language.

S---, I thought to myself, still pretending to be asleep. Were we at our apartment? Did Maal want to drop me off first? So he could be alone with

Anna?

I did not dare open my eyes, even the slightest bit.

"*Pax, you idiot,*" Maal said, still in our language. "*Get the f--- out of the car.*"

Still I remained perfectly still, like I had heard nothing. Inside the car was quiet.

"I know what should do to wake Prince Charm," Anna said. I could hear her moving around in her seat. "It simple," she said, her voice much closer, like she was facing me, like she was leaning over the back of her seat toward me. "All I do is kiss him awake."

My eyes shot open.

Anna had climbed half way over her seat. Her face was very close to mine and moving closer, her lips ready to kiss me.

I pushed away from the door, threw my body across the seat toward the center of the car—the only way I could go to avoid Anna's lips.

Her eyes, her whole face went blank with shock and hurt. "I no di*sease*," she said.

Maal laughed loudly. "There goes your Prince Charming."

TWENTY FOUR

I stared at Anna. How could she try to kiss me? Right there in front of Maal? How drunk was she? To do something that would make him so angry?

Maal spoke calmly in our language. *"Get the f--- out of the f---ing car."*

I sat back and crossed my arms. *"You need to take her home first,"* I said, not looking at either one of them.

"Lucky for me," Maal said, still speaking our language, *"you don't get to tell me what the f--- to do. Now get out of the car before I go upstairs and get one of my father's guns and blow your balls off."*

I did not move a muscle. *"She is enwaa."*

"F--- you. She's not enwaa."

"What wrong?" Anna asked, hearing the anger in Maal's voice.

Maal spoke in English. "He thinks you're a little girl."

"*Me?*" Anna's eyes grew large. "I no little girl."

I still hadn't moved. "*She is enwaa and she is drunk.*"

"*What the f--- do you think I'm going to do? Now get out of the f---ing car.*"

Anna raised her voice. "I no little girl."

I looked at her. I realized all I had left to protect her with was the truth. I pointed at her, jabbing my finger, and then held up ten fingers and then held up another five fingers.

"I fifteen," she agreed. "But I almost sixteen! Almost your age."

I shook my head.

"*Pax, shut up,*" Maal said, in our language.

I waved a finger between Maal and me, pointing to the two of us.

"*Pax, don't.*"

I looked at Anna and held up ten fingers, then held up nine fingers.

"What?" Anna cried. "*Nineteen?* You not nineteen."

I nodded.

Anna looked at Maal. "You nineteen?"

Maal breathed a deep breath and said nothing.

Anna smiled. "You two *NINETEEN?*"

I could hear in her voice that I had made a mistake. I had thought that Anna would be intimidated when she heard Maal and I were nineteen. But she was not the least bit intimidated.

"I with nineteen year old men!" Anna was happy. She *liked* it that we were four years older than she was.

"See?" Maal said, in English. "Everything's OK."

"Everything OK," Anna agreed.

I crossed my arms again, still determined. "*Ask her if she's enwaa.*"

"*What the f--- are you talking about? Americans do not understand enwaa.*"

"*Ask her if she thinks she is ready to have sex.*"

Maal slipped into English. "F--- you."

"What wrong?" Anna looked from Maal to me.

"He thinks you're a little girl," Maal said. "He thinks you're a drunk little girl."

Anna laughed. "*Drunk?*" Her voice was too loud. "Please. I no drunk."

"See?" Maal said, gripping the steering wheel, his knuckles white. He spoke softly but I could hear the danger in his voice. "Now would you please tell Pax to get out of the car so I can drive you home?"

Anna reached back and patted my knee. "I no drunk," she said. "I fine."

"See?" Maal kept speaking English. "You need to leave now, Pax."

Anna nodded. "It OK."

It was my turn to breathe a deep breath. I did not know what to do.

Maal growled in our language. "*Get. Out.*"

"Please," Anna said. "I no want fight. You go. I OK."

I still did not know what to do.

"*Please*," Anna said, again, watching, holding her breath. "For me."

I looked at Anna's soft eyes. And made the worst decision of my life.

TWENTY FIVE

I do not remember getting out of the car. I remember sitting in the backseat, unsure of what to do. And I remember standing outside and hesitating before closing the door, trying to think of something I could do, anything I could do. Once I was out of the car, though, it was too late. Even if I had tried to climb back in, Maal would have driven the car away before I would have been able to get inside.

I closed the door, and Maal quickly pulled away. Watching the red tail lights, my stomach felt empty, but I was not hungry. A cold wind pushed at me as I watched the car get smaller. Then it turned left and disappeared. I kept standing there. What would Poppy have done? I stood there and asked him. What would you have done, Poppy? I really wanted to know, but Poppy would not tell me. I did not feel him there at all, and for the first time in my life, I believed he was right. I believed there was no God. It was probably not fair to God, but I thought if there was a God, He or She would let Poppy talk to me as I stood on the cold deserted street. God would have insisted that Poppy tell me *something*. But all I could feel was the cold wind, pushing and pulling at me.

It was a long way up the three flights to the apartment. I was glad Maal's father would not be home until very late from the restaurant. Street light was pouring in through the open blinds, throwing stripes up on the ceiling. For some reason I did not turn on any lights. I walked carefully in the near darkness and pulled out my bed from under Maal's bed and lay down on the blanket with all my clothes on, even my shoes. I lay there on my back, staring up at the stripes on the ceiling. And, very quietly, I began to cry. I shut my eyes, but still the tears escaped. I remember asking myself why I was crying.

I was not sure, I told myself, but I worried that I knew exactly why I was crying. I crossed my arms and pulled them tight against my body, trying to pray to anyone who might listen to not let it be so.

I was trying to pray when my phone rang.

I jumped and sat up. The phone I carried in my pocket had never done anything, but now it was ringing and buzzing and seemed like a small wild animal when I pulled it out my pocket. I did not know how to use it, but I had seen Maal pull it open like a clamshell, and so that is what I did. The ringing and buzzing stopped, and I held the phone to my ear.

"Pax?" I heard Maal shout. "Pax, are you there, you stupid s---?"

"*Is everything all right?*" I asked, in my language.

"Everything is *great*," Maal called out, his voice loud and fast, like he had had a great deal of coffee. "Anna has something she wants to tell you.

Tell him, Anna."

"*Please.*" Anna's voice sounded far away.

"Hear her begging for it? Hear it? Tell Pax what you want. Tell Prince Charming."

"Don't. *No.* Please." Anna cried out like a small animal caught in the jaws of a hawk. My body squeezed tight, hearing her pain.

"*Say it,*" Maal growled. "Say what you want."

"I want you," Anna said quickly, like she needed the words to be out of her mouth.

"What do you want?" Maal asked. "This is what you want. Tell him this is what you want. Tell him you want *this.*"

"Oh, God, please no."

"*Maal, stop,*" I said.

"Tell Prince Charming what you want inside you."

"*Maal, do not do this.*"

"Ask for it," Maal said. "Beg for it."

Anna screamed. "*Please please stop.*"

"*MAAL,*" I shouted into the small phone.
"*STOP!*"

"No moving!" Maal called out. "I told you no
moving."

"*I no move,*" Anna pleaded. "*I no move. Please
no. PLEASE!*"

"I know you want it."

"*Please no.*"

"You want it."

"*NOOOOOO!*" I screamed.

"Here it is, you slut."

Anna cried out again, a shrieking gasp of
pain.

I closed the phone, threw it away from me. A
coward. I was a coward, could not hear anymore. I
stood up, my throat tight, my fists clenched with
helplessness. I needed to find them. I needed to try.
I fell to my knees at the dresser and in a few seconds

stuffed everything I owned into my sack. Without thinking I slid across the floor and reached under the gun cabinet and pulled out the photograph of Maal sitting in his mother's lap with his baby sister. Later I would wonder what made me think of taking it, but at the time I just stuffed it into my sack as I stood up and leapt for the door. I ran down the stairs so fast that I lost track of my feet and had to grab hold of the handrail to avoid falling. Outside I ran as fast as I could down the street and took the left I remembered Maal taking in the car. The side street was narrow and dark, the streetlight slipping through the dead looking branches of the trees overhead. I was stupid to run as fast as I could because soon I was out of my breath and needed to slow down and suck in air. I ran more slowly, looking up and down the streets I passed. My legs felt heavy, like I had been carrying a great weight, and soon the small hope I had of finding them began to disappear somewhere ahead of me. I had no choice but to keep moving, to keep trying, but soon I lost heart and the only thing that kept me running was knowing how miserable I would feel when I stopped running, when I gave up.

Eventually, I was sweating so much that I took off my ugly jacket with the fake fur and could see steam coming off my body in the cold. I kept walking, kept looking, but I knew much time had passed and I would be too late. Why did I get out of the car? I asked myself a thousand times that night, each time cursing myself for being so stupid. I could feel blisters on the backs of my heels and welcomed them, the pain less than I deserved.

The streets were all deserted now, so I was surprised when a car stopped beside me and a man stuck his head out of the passenger window and asked if I had any money. I did not answer, just kept walking, and the car drove slowly beside me and other voices from inside the car called out to me. My heart pounded with fear, but I was not going to run away. I knew if these men did something to me, if they hurt me, it would be no more than I deserved. If they got out the car with a knife and stabbed me, it would be no more than I deserved. Let them come, I thought. It was only fair.

But they did not come. Instead they got bored with calling out to me and drove away. I kept walking, my legs rubbery, my feet swollen, wondering why they had not gotten out of the car. I asked myself why I had been left alone, what was I left to do, and when the answer came to me, I was disappointed in myself for not seeing it sooner.

I turned around and began to run again, slowly because I knew I had a long way to go. If I could find my way back to the apartment, then I thought I could also find my way to where I needed to go. Several times I had thought I had lost my way, and even when I eventually found the street where Maal and his father lived, I was not sure I was headed in the right direction, and I asked Poppy, if he was still somewhere, to please help guide me to where I needed to go.

At the next corner I thought I smelled coffee. I took another sniff. Definitely coffee. I walked faster and quickly found the bright pink and white lights of the donut shop.

I crossed the street before reaching the shop, did not want to be tempted by the warmth inside, by the dizzying smell of hot coffee. I walked to Anna's building and sat on the steps, my legs happy to rest even though the coldness of the stone step pushed through my pants. It was possible, I knew, that Anna was already home, but I believed she was still out, and I was ready to wait a long time for her to be sure. I was very glad for my ugly jacket—it felt colder without walking. For a long time I avoided looking across the street at the donut shop. I had $7.36 in my pocket, which I was pretty sure was enough to buy a coffee, but I did not feel like I deserved to drink hot coffee. How could I drink hot coffee when I knew what had happened to Anna?

I began to get angry again, remembering the phone call. I needed to stop Maal. I wished I had the courage to kill Maal, because I hated him enough to kill him, but I did not believe that I could do it. Even if I had a gun, I would hesitate, thinking about the gunshot entering into his body and ripping it apart. I would hesitate to pull the trigger, and Maal would have his chance to kill me, and I would be dead. Without accomplishing anything.

I did not want to kill him. I could not do it. I knew it was wrong to kill someone who was not attacking me or my family.

Even if he enjoyed attacking teenage girls.

I did not believe I could succeed in killing

Maal. But I needed to do everything, anything I could to stop him from doing this again. I needed to get him away from other girls. I needed to find some way of getting Maal in jail.

The anger that built inside my heart distracted me from my determination to sit and wait for Anna. I began to look at the pink and white lights of the donut shop, began to imagine sipping hot coffee. I battled with myself for a long time, but it was a battle I eventually lost.

I stood up and walked across the deserted street. When I went through the door it was brighter inside than out, and the warmth that surrounded me made me want to cry. The shop was empty, and as soon as I walked in the woman behind the counter smiled and asked if she could help me. I was stupid, at first, and thought she somehow knew I was in trouble and needed help, but then I realized she just wanted to know what I wanted to buy.

I pointed to a stack of upside down cups.

"Latte?" the woman asked.

I did not know this word and got nervous, looked away from the woman. I looked out the window, across the street, to make sure no one was there.

"Coffee?" the woman asked.

I nodded quickly and took money out of my pocket to prove I could pay. The woman filled the cup with coffee. I could feel my mouth fill with saliva, looking at the steam rising from the cup.

"Cream and sugar?" the woman asked.

I did not know what coffee with cream would taste like. I was tempted to ask for sugar, but then I thought of Poppy and wanted the taste of coffee, dark and bitter and full of life. I shook my head to the cream and sugar and the woman took some of the money I had left on the counter. I nodded thank you to the woman and stuffed the rest of my money into my pocket and looked back across the street. There was no one at the small tables, and I could have sat in the warmth and kept a look out for Anna, but that did not feel right to me, after what I had done.

I walked back out into the cold and crossed the abandoned street and sat on the steps of Anna's building. The coffee tasted thin compared to the coffee Poppy and I would make, but it was delicious and wonderfully hot. I held my fingers over the cup and let the steam coming out of the lid warm them. Poppy claimed he had his best ideas early in the morning, sipping coffee, and so I stared into the space ahead of me and tried to think of what I could do. As the coffee cooled, I drank more quickly, my mind running hard, thinking about *jalil* and what choices we make that allow life to be easier or harder. This was not about Maal, I seemed to realize all at once, like someone had whispered it my ear.

This was about me, and choices *I* had made. Even sitting there on the cold steps, I had choices— choices that would lead me in different directions. And as soon as I realized this, or as soon as I remembered this, I felt a wave of bumps rush along my skin because I knew what I needed to do.

I needed to find some way to make up for what I had done.

I needed to speak against Maal.

This was what I realized when I saw a police car drive slowly down the street and stop in front of me.

TWENTY SIX

Anna was in the backseat of the police car and looked away when she saw me.

Both doors opened quickly on the other side of the car and a female police officer jumped out of back seat door while the older police officer who was driving climbed out more slowly. The female police officer walked quickly around behind the car, looking at me.

"Who are you?" she called.

I said nothing. I saw her look at the other police officer, who spoke loudly.

"Hey, buddy, the lady asked you a question."

I did not move. In my country, everyone knows that you do not want to do anything that might give someone carrying a gun a reason to shoot.

The woman opened Anna's door half way

and leaned down to talk to her quietly. The older officer walked slowly around the front of the car, never taking his eyes off me. The female officer stood back up.

"This is the brother."

The older officer looked at me and sighed. "What are you doing here?"

As Anna climbed out of the car, she had her coat wrapped tightly around herself, the hood draped over her face. The white knuckles of her fist holding the jacket to her throat made me feel like she would never be able to let go again. "*It not his fault*," she called.

"She keeps saying that," the older officer said. "It's not your fault, son."

"Pax good to me," Anna insisted. Her head was bowed, but I saw her eyes look up at me. "You good."

I shook my head, stepping down to the

sidewalk. I struggled to speak the only English words that had ever come out of my mouth. "I sorry."

"No, Pax, *no*." Anna started to cry. "My fault."

The female officer put her arm around Anna. "Honey, none of this is your fault. Do you hear me? *None of it.* You need to remember that."

"Not Pax fault," Anna said, gasping for air as she cried. "I too scared to fight back."

I had to bite my teeth hard against each other to not cry.

"Your brother's going to walk free," the older cop said, quietly, looking down at his shiny black shoes. He sounded ashamed.

"Maal tell police I *want* it," Anna cried out, sobbing. "I say no. No, no, *no*."

"We know the truth," the female officer said, holding Anna. "We know."

I needed to do something. I could not walk away from this. I looked at the older police officer. I was still holding the coffee cup, but I held my arms out in front of me and pressed my wrists together and walked toward the older police officer, turning myself in, ready for him to handcuff me.

"Pax," Anna called, "what you do?"

The older cop eyed me suspiciously. "What the hell are you doing, kid? She said you tried to save her."

I shook my wrists at him.

"*No, Pax.*" Anna was nearly shouting. "Not your fault."

The older cop was shaking his head. "I can't arrest you, kid. You haven't done anything wrong."

For a moment I was worried they were going to let me walk free, just like Maal. Then I looked at the coffee cup in my hand, and I looked at the older officer, and I threw the cup at his shoes, the plastic lid flying off, the black liquid inside splashing up on the officer's pants.

TWENTY SEVEN

I was not as stupid as the older police officer thought I was when he handcuffed me. I did not throw a coffee cup at him to get arrested. I threw a coffee cup at him because I needed to tell the police what I knew— I needed to tell the police that Maal had committed *falil* and needed to be locked away.

But that night at the police station I could tell them nothing but yes and no. There was no one who spoke my language, and even though the police had my passport and knew where I came from, they said it would be a day or two until they could find someone who could understand me.

They asked me many questions, however, and I listened and nodded my head and shook my head and lost my heart. Maal had already been released, I learned. He would be going to school on Monday. There was nothing they could do because

Maal and the lawyer his father bought claimed the sexual relations had been *consensual*, which I found out meant Anna had agreed to have sexual relations. Since I was not there when it happened, the police told me that what I said would not be enough to prove that Maal had forced himself on Anna.

The only time I had hope was when they asked me about my age. Anna had told them what I had said in the car, that Maal and I were nineteen. The police asked me if that was true. They said that in America, a nineteen year old cannot have sexual relations with a fifteen year old, and that if they could prove that Maal was nineteen, then he would go to jail.

At first they seemed excited when they asked me if Maal was nineteen and I nodded yes. But their excitement went away quickly because I did not have proof. My passport said I was sixteen. Maal's passport said he was sixteen. What proof did I have that this was not true?

The police poured me another cup of coffee and left me alone. I tried to think how I could prove Maal was nineteen. It seemed impossible, without his certificate of birth. I was sure that Maal's father would have gotten rid of any original copies they might have had of Maal's certificate of birth. And the record office had burned down several years ago, so there was no way to get a new copy.

But—

I looked up, a spark of hope shooting off in my heart.

There *was* something Maal's father may not have thought of.

Getting a copy of Maal's certificate of birth seemed impossible.

But it might not be impossible to get his dead sister's certificate of birth.

His sister would have been sixteen, if she had

lived. Her certificate of birth would show her being born two months before Maal's certificate of birth claimed he was born. If I could get a copy of his sister's certificate of birth, I could prove that Maal's passport was wrong. And maybe people would realize he was lying, and that I was telling the truth that he was nineteen.

But how could I get Maal's sister's certificate of birth when I could trust no one and his father had friends in many places? I doubted Maal's mother, if she had her daughter's certificate of birth, would give it away. Particularly if she found out it might mean Maal would go to jail. I could try to contact someone in the village and ask them to try to get it away from Maal's mother, but even if they could, getting the certificate of birth here to America would require trusting many people.

I stared down at what was left of my coffee, the black liquid cold now. It reminded me of the inky look of the sea when Poppy would take me out fishing before dawn. As a little boy, I was scared of catching a fish in the darkness. I would worry that instead of me pulling the fish out, the fish would pull me in and I would disappear into the black water.

"What if the fish is stronger than I am?" I remembered asking Poppy one chilly morning when the water looked especially black. I could see Poppy's white teeth as he smiled in the darkness.

"You do not need to be stronger than the fish," Poppy told me. "You just need to convince the fish that you are stronger."

I looked up from my empty cup of coffee.

Maybe I did not need the certificate of birth.

Maybe I just needed to convince someone that I had the certificate of birth.

Someone I knew.

Someone I could trust.

There was one person I knew well enough to trust. If I could convince this person that I had the certificate of birth, it was possible that I could make up, at least a little bit, for my *falil*.

My heart started to beat hard. My plan would require me to be braver than I had ever been in my life, and my stomach flopped like a fish in the bottom of the boat. Not only would I need to testify in court.

But I would have one chance and one chance only.

TWENTY EIGHT

That is it. That is my story, as far as I know it.

I spent the next day in the police station, and it was dark again when they took me here to the detention center. When they brought me to this room, I looked at the only window, up high, where I can see a small chink of sky. It was black when I got here.

And it is black again now. It feels like I have been staring at the window for hours, waiting for the sky to stop being black. I am waiting for the sky to lighten, and I am hoping that Mrs. LaVenya brings coffee because I think coffee will give me courage.

Of all the days of my life, today I need courage.

Because today I testify.

My mouth is dry, like I had too much to

drink. If I do not have children, this will be the most important day of my life, the most important thing I will ever do.

There are two thoughts that terrify me.

One is that my testimony will not convince the one person I need to convince.

The other is that Maal and his father will stop me from testifying. There is only one way they could do that. But I know if they can, they will.

Mrs. LaVenya will collect the recorder of sound today, so this is the last thing I can say. I would like to thank Mrs. LaVenya for the kindness in her eyes, and I would like to thank Poppy for sending me to America to tell my story.

PART TWO
Mrs. LaVenya

TWENTY NINE

Roddy Martinez from the night shift laughed when he saw everything I was carrying that Friday morning— two jumbo breakfasts, a half dozen donuts, and two of the largest cups they had from the fancy coffee place. "The kid must have quite an appetite."

"It's his last day in America," I pointed out. "He should have what he wants for breakfast."

Roddy looked at his watch. "He might not even be up yet."

"He's up."

Roddy thought about it, then finally got up out of his seat so we could go get Pax. "How much you end up collecting for him?"

"Nine hundred and twelve."

"Holy s---!" Roddy squinted. "How much were people kicking in?"

"More than you did, I can tell you that."

"Hey, you try telling your pregnant wife that you're giving money to an illegal alien who's being deported."

We were walking side by side, headed down the hall toward the north wing. We reached a door Roddy had to unlock. He held it open for me.

"Did Doc Z really put a hit on him?"

Doc Z was one of the top crime bosses in Connecticut. Maal's father was a thug for Doc Z, which meant that if someone messed with Maal's father or anyone in his family, it would be a personal insult to Doc Z. People tried very hard not to insult Doc Z.

"That's why they moved up the trial," I said. "They think Pax's best chance of getting out of America alive is getting on a plane as soon as possible."

"And you figured the nine hundred bucks

might help him disappear."

"The kid's completely on his own. I had to do something."

Roddy looked over at me as we walked. "Hey, how much of that nine hundred was yours?"

I shrugged, wouldn't look at him. "Enough."

We walked in silence the rest of the way to Pax's cell. Roddy put the key into the door, but then stopped. He took his wallet out of his back pocket, opened it up, and handed me a twenty.

"Do me a favor and don't tell anyone," he said. "I don't want it getting back to the wife."

I started getting choked up and had to fight it off. All morning it had been the same. My dog Binny looked at me sitting at the kitchen table, not drinking my coffee, not moving. When he came over to comfort me by putting his head in my lap, I burst into tears.

"Thanks, Roddy," I said, swallowing hard to

avoid crying. "I won't say a word to anyone. But I also won't forget this."

THIRTY

Roddy opened the door. Pax was standing in the middle of the room, facing us.

"The coffee smells good," he said, trying to smile.

He looked nervous. The knot in my throat made a strange sound. The three of us walked back to the interrogation room. The suit District Attorney Salinger had ordered for Pax to wear in court was hung up on the back of the door. I was glad I knew how to tie a man's tie because I was sure Pax did not.

I laid out the food on the table as Pax sat across from me and watched. He waited until I had finished before trying his coffee.

"It's from a fancy place," I said, just talking to have something to say. "I thought since you wanted it black, maybe you would notice the difference."

Pax smiled. *"It is the best cup of coffee I have ever had."*

We looked at each other, but then I had to look away to avoid more tears. There was something I wanted to say, and I knew I needed to say it now or I would never manage to say it. "If I had had a son," I blurted out, saying the words as fast as I could, "I would have wanted—" My throat closed. I shut my eyes and held my forehead to hide the tears. "I would have wanted him to turn out like you."

Pax said nothing. I moved my hand covering my eyes enough to look at him. He had a hand on his forehead as well, covering his eyes. I heard him sniffle.

"Pax—"

"I am such a coward."

"Because you're scared?" I asked, in his language. *"You'd be a fool not to be scared."*

Pax's shoulders heaved a sob. I tried to think

of something to distract him.

"*I brought the colored paper you asked for,*" I said, opening my large green purse and taking out a manila folder. "*Red, green, blue and yellow. That's what you wanted, yes?*"

Pax nodded, still hiding his eyes.

I had no idea what the paper was for, but I did not want to ask Pax anything at the moment. When you're crying, you don't want to be answering a lot of questions.

"*Try the hotcakes,*" I said, in his language, reaching over and pulling open the syrup container. "*Dip them in the syrup and see what you think. The sausage is greasy but delicious.*"

I kept talking, which is what I do when I'm nervous, and eventually I got Pax to stop crying and try the hotcakes. He said they were good, but then put the plastic fork down and just drank his coffee. I sipped some of my coffee as well.

"*I was curious,*" I said, "*so I ordered my coffee black, no sugar.*"

"*What do you think?*" Pax asked.

I sipped more coffee. "*I think I like cream and sugar.*"

Pax nodded, not like he agreed but like he understood. "*I am used to the bitterness,*" he said. "*Poppy used to say that coffee without sugar has the richness of jalil.*"

"*I do not understand,*" I said. "*That makes jalil sound like a good thing. How can the hardship of life be a good thing?*"

"*I do not think Poppy would say jalil is good,*" Pax said, thinking it out as he spoke. "*I think he would say that it is part of the full circle of life.*"

I took another sip off coffee. It was true that without the cream and sugar, the sharp flavor of the coffee took over my mouth. "*I have something for you,*" I told Pax. I reached into my purse and took out the thick white envelope. I slipped in the twenty that Roddy had just given me and tucked the flap inside the envelope and handed it to Pax.

He opened the flap and saw the money inside and quickly put the envelope down on the table. He turned away. "*What is it you want me to do?*"

"*Nothing!*" I said. It had not occurred to me that Pax would think I was trying to bribe him, but perhaps in his country that would be the only reason to give someone a large sum of money. "*I am not trying to get you to do anything, Pax. A bunch of us just wanted to make sure you had some cash to get back on your feet in your country.*"

Pax looked from me to the envelope.

"*I thought you could find a new village and have enough money to buy a hut and a boat.*"

Pax smiled and pointed to the envelope. "*In my country, the only thing that much money would get me is dead.*"

I didn't understand. Pax explained that that much money would get noticed by the military checking people at the airport. They would detain him and take the money and might kill him if they thought he would tell someone. And if by some miracle he was able to get through the airport with the money, he could not show up in a village where he knew no one and start buying things. Someone in the village would see that he was rich and would slit his throat in the night.

"It is safer to be poor in my country," Pax said. *"No one can take from you what you do not have."*

He eventually agreed to take two fifty dollar bills—one for each shoe. It was probably more than was safe, he said, but he could get a bus to take him far out of the city, where he hoped to find a village where he could get everyone drunk and make them think he knew how to get more money.

"It is not safe to have money," he said, smiling.

"But people will respect you if they think you know how to steal it."

We drank our coffee and nibbled on donuts as Pax told me stories about Poppy talking to the priest about God. It was as if we were able to forget, for a little while, what day it was.

Then there was a loud knock on the door, and someone—I didn't even recognize the voice—called to us through the door.

"Salinger wants him dressed and ready to go."

Pax and I looked at each other. We both knew that, no matter what happened, our time together was over.

THIRTY ONE

Hurry up and wait. That's the way it works with courts—you have to be ready to go, but the judge can have you wait hours until he or she is ready for you.

Detectives Patterson and Wilson showed up while Pax was getting dressed. I was surprised at how jealous I felt when Patterson tied Pax's tie for him. I was also surprised at how handsome Pax looked. For some reason the suit made him look like a different person—like he had graduated college and was waiting for a job interview.

The four of us sat around the table in the interrogation room. And we sat. And we sat. Wilson and Patterson both had two donuts, and I eventually finished my cold hotcakes.

Patterson explained to Pax that there would be five of us taking him to the court house—myself,

Detectives Wilson and Patterson, and Officers Coleman and O'Malley, the two police officers who drove him to the station that first night. All five of us had requested to be there because we didn't want to risk a friend of Maal's father somehow figuring out a way to sign up for the job.

Pax sat there with his arms crossed and spoke in his language without looking at me. "*Could you please tell them that I don't want you coming with us to the courthouse?*"

"*I'm already scheduled,*" I told him.

Pax shook his head. "*I do not want you there.*"

"*Thank you, Pax, but luckily for me, you do not get to make that decision.*"

He looked at me, held my gaze. "*Please,*" he asked.

"What does he want?" Patterson asked, sitting across from Pax.

"*Pax.*" I kept my voice calm even though I

176

didn't feel calm. "*I am the only person I trust to understand what you are saying,*" I told him. "*If I was not there, and something happened, I would feel like I had committed falil.*"

Pax looked back down at the table because he knew he had no response for this. He could not ask me to do something that could lead me to commit *falil*. But he was not happy.

"Look," Patterson said, "it's going to be fine. We will take you out through the garage, and at the courthouse, we will park just outside the back entrance and have you inside the building in less than ten seconds."

Pax said nothing for a long while. "*I would like to be alone before we go.*"

THIRTY TWO

Patterson, Wilson and I left Pax alone in the interrogation room. I was not about to go anywhere, however. I grabbed a chair and parked myself outside the door. No one was going to get into that room unless I knew who they were.

Both Patterson and Wilson were apparently thinking the same thing because they found their own chairs and joined me. Wilson played some game on his phone, but Patterson and I just sat there.

"Scared?" he asked me.

"Terrified," I admitted. I had never in my twenty-five year career escorted a witness with a bounty on his head.

"We can handle this," Patterson said. "You don't need to be there."

"I need to be there."

He took a deep loud breath. "What about

your husband?"

"I don't talk about my husband."

"Does he know you're doing this?"

"Patterson, you have three kids who are hoping Daddy comes home tonight. Don't try to tell me who the hell should and shouldn't be here. Now if you don't mind, I'd prefer we talk about something else."

Wilson looked up from his game. "How about we talk about that piece of crap Knicks? How about someone tell me why the hell they can't score points?"

Patterson bowed his head in resignation. I stared straight ahead at a gray wall. I was staying with Pax as long as I could—had gotten assigned to be with him until he was on that plane headed home. I'd lived alone for more years than I wanted to count. I knew people from work and even considered some of them friends, but until I'd met

Pax, the most intimate conversations I had had were with my dog Binny. I enjoyed my job as interpreter, had learned nine languages to do it, but in my adult life I had not cared about anything more than I did about the end of Pax's story. I wasn't sure if I believed in God, but I believed in Pax's dying mother. I believed that if she wanted him to come to America to tell his story, I was going to do everything in my power to make sure it had a happy ending.

Patterson's phone buzzed. He pulled it out of his pocket at looked at it. "Game time."

Wilson got on his phone to let Coleman and O'Malley know we were on our way. The plan was the three of us would escort Pax down in the elevator, and Coleman and O'Malley would meet us down in the basement garage with their cruiser running.

When we opened the door to the

interrogation room, I could not look at Pax, did not want to focus on what he was feeling or thinking. He was a witness and it was my job to make sure he was safe. I needed to stay focused on the job.

Wilson got Pax to take off his suit jacket and strapped him into a bullet proof vest. With the jacket back on, Pax looked twenty pounds heavier. We walked quickly to the elevator, my eyes everywhere, trying to see everything all at once. I kept getting the sense that someone was watching us, but that was craziness because no one was there.

On the elevator no one spoke, but we all stood at attention, as if we expected something to happen. Wilson had his hand under his suit jacket, ready to draw his gun.

Coleman was standing there when the elevator doors opened. She had her gun in her right hand, the barrel pointed at the ground. She walked behind the rest of us as we marched in a cluster toward the police cruiser. We got Pax positioned in the middle of the backseat, between me and Patterson. Wilson and Coleman squeezed into the front seat, where O'Malley was already waiting behind the wheel.

We had decided not to go through the center of town to avoid stop and go traffic that might make us more vulnerable. Instead we took the highway—it was twice as long but there was an exit a block from the courthouse.

O'Malley didn't waste any time. He drove fast and did not stop for red lights. I didn't realize I was holding my breath until we got on the highway and I could breathe more easily. All we had to do now was get Pax into the courthouse and he would be safe.

But there was a backup when we got off the exit.

"What the f---?" Wilson asked, sitting up,

trying to see what the holdup was about.

"Hit the siren," Patterson told O'Malley.

"Get us the f--- out of here," Wilson agreed.

Officer O'Malley turned on the lights and siren, which sounded louder than I would have thought inside the police car. At first, nothing happened because the cars ahead of us had no where they could go, but O'Malley squeezed over to the left and slowly the cars ahead of us pulled over to the right. As we got close to the courthouse—a large, gray, windowless building—we saw what the problem was. Just beyond the courthouse, two men were out of their cars, arguing and pointing to where their two cars had collided. When the day was done, I would regret not asking someone to get their license plates, but at the time I was too focused on still being a half block from the back entrance of the courthouse and not moving. We were all antsy, sitting there in the car, and Wilson and Patterson decided that we would get out now and walk the extra few steps.

"Whatever the f--- happens," Wilson said, "we don't stop."

All four doors popped open and we all climbed out, Patterson grabbing Pax by the arm as Coleman ran ahead of us, walking backwards, looking up and down the street, all of us moving fast, closing in on the entrance to the courtroom.

We had less than ten feet to go when the shots rang out—two shots, not loud. Later we would learn that the shots were fired from a rooftop 252 feet away, but when it happened my head spun because I wasn't even sure what it was.

Then I saw Pax go down.

THIRTY THREE

His left leg seemed to collapse and I saw blood splatter on the sidewalk. It was bright red and I was shocked that I could smell it. People were screaming, and Wilson and Patterson had a hold of Pax and were half carrying, half dragging him toward the entrance, O'Malley and Coleman with their guns out, scanning the street with jumpy eyes, trying to spot the gunman. I yanked the door open for Wilson and Patterson and saw Pax's face squeezed tight with pain as the two detectives pulled him inside, leaving a smear of bright red on the ground.

Three policemen raced outside, guns drawn, and an overweight guard had opened a wheel chair as other guards shouted for people to stay down, to move away from the windows. Wilson and Patterson gently slipped Pax into the wheelchair. Pax bent over, holding his wounded leg. He'd been hit in the thigh. Wilson tore his own jack off and wrapped it around Pax's thigh and pulled it tight. Pax groaned in pain.

"Gotta stop the bleeding," Wilson said.

"We need an ambulance," I called out, my voice quivering like I was about to cry.

"No," Pax said, shaking his head.

I grabbed his hand and squeezed it. "*We'll make sure it's safe, Pax. I promise.*"

Pax kept shaking his head. "*I want to testify.*"

"*You will,*" I said.

"*Now,*" he said, groaning again.

"*Pax. We need to stop the bleeding.*"

Pax was still leaning over his wounded leg. "*It has to be now,*" he said.

"Pax—"

"*Now!*" he shouted, and then looked at me, his face tight with pain. "*Please,*" he pleaded. "*My leg is fine. It has stopped bleeding.*"

Patterson kept his head down and his gun drawn as he ran over to the three of us.

"What the hell's going on?" he asked.

"He wants to testify," I said. "Now. Before we go to the hospital."

"Who the f--- can blame him?" Wilson asked. "How do we know the shooter isn't still the f--- out there?"

I was having a hard time breathing and kept telling myself not to cry, not to cry.

Patterson looked at Pax's leg. The drops of blood had stopped dripping onto the floor, but all I could think about was making Pax safe.

"We need to get him to the hospital."

"We can't get the f--- out of here until it's secure," Wilson said. "How long's that going to take? If he testifies now, we won't have to go through this s--- again."

Patterson's eyes kept darting around, like he

was looking for an answer. "Let's get someone looking at his leg to make sure the bleeding's stopped."

Wilson nodded. "I'll go tell Judge Banks he's got to f---ing expedite."

"*I need to do this,*" Pax said.

"*OK, OK.*" I was down on my knees, clutching the side of the wheelchair. "*We're trying.*"

A young guy with a black bag came over to look at the leg. He tried moving it gently, and Pax's face squeezed tight with pain.

"The bleeding's stopped," he said. "He should be OK until they secure the area."

"How long will it take?" I asked.

"Your guess is as good as mine."

I glared at Patterson. "How long will it take to secure the area?"

"I don't know for sure," he said, "but longer than it would take him to testify."

I shook my head, still didn't like the idea.

"*Please*," Pax said, through gritted teeth. "*Take me upstairs.*"

I could see Patterson looking at me, wanting to know what Pax had said. "They will notify you," I said, pointing at Patterson, holding on tight to the side of the wheelchair, "as soon as the area is secure and we can get out of here?"

He nodded.

"And we'll get him out immediately, even if he hasn't finished testifying?"

"Promise."

I looked at Pax. He looked pale, his body slumped over his injured leg. I didn't want to do this, didn't want to think about anything but getting Pax safe. "S---," I said, and looked at Patterson. "You push. I'll make sure he doesn't fall out of the damn chair."

THIRTY FOUR

Patterson wheeled Pax to the elevator. One of the guards held the door. Pax groaned when the wheelchair bumped slightly crossing the gap, getting onto the elevator. I winced, imagining the pain he was feeling, and kept watching his leg. If I saw any sign of more bleeding, I was calling the whole thing off and we were getting Pax out of there.

The elevator was so slow I started getting angry. *Come on, come on.* When the doors finally opened, I reached over and wrapped my arm around Pax's shoulder, ready to hold him up if I had to. He remained motionless, leaning against the arm of the chair as Wilson wheeled him down the wide hallway. Security must have been warned we were coming because there were guards everywhere, including two who held the doors open for us. Patterson wheeled Pax into the courtroom, the rows of seats mostly empty but both judge and jury seated up front.

"Oh, God. Pax!"

I looked up and saw Anna, standing in the first row to the right, behind the prosecution table. Her face was tight with fear, looking at Pax as Patterson wheeled the chair past her. I had seen photographs of Anna but had not seen her in person. She had a small frame and did not even look fifteen. I shivered to think of what Maal had done to her, and it brought tears to my eyes, hearing her concern for Pax.

A lawyer at the defense table stood up and spoke loudly.

"Your honor, I'm sure you see how this biases the jury against my client."

I was furious. How could he dare talk about what was fair or unfair to his client. His client's father hired someone to kill Pax in order to stop him from testifying. And now—because Pax had been shot—Maal's lawyer was trying to claim that the jury would see a young man bleeding in a wheel chair and judge against his client.

With all my heart I wanted to slap his face.

"Your honor!" Salinger was at the defense table and shouted over Maal's lawyer's voice. "This is outrageous! How can the defense—"

The judge pounded his gavel. "One more word from either one of you and I'll hold you in contempt. This young man has generously agreed to testify before being treated for his wound—"

"But your honor—" This came from a female lawyer at the defense table, standing up. "Clearly this will prejudice the jury in favor of his testimony."

"Counselor, a gunshot wound will have no impact on what the jury hears. There will be no further discussion. I'm giving each side five minutes with the witness while we wait for an ambulance team to safely make it into the building so this young man can be treated as soon as possible. Constable, please swear in the witness."

Patterson had brought the wheelchair in front of the witness stand, and had carefully turned Pax around to face the courtroom. I turned and stood beside him, facing the courtroom. For the first time, my eyes scanned faces, and the first one I stopped at was Maal's. He was glaring at Pax as if he hoped to cause him further bodily harm. His jaw tightened and re-tightened, his body perfectly still but tense, like it was set on a spring.

"Do you swear to tell the truth, the whole truth, and nothing but the truth?"

Pax was still slumped over against the side of the wheelchair, his hand held over the wound in his leg. He raised his head and nodded. "*Yes*," he said, in his language.

"Yes!" I translated, speaking more loudly than I need to.

Salinger walked slowly toward us as he spoke. "Pax, I wanted to thank you for being willing to testify despite a gunshot tearing your leg open."

"Objection," the young defense lawyer called out, standing.

The judge pointed at Salinger. "Don't waste your five minutes, counselor, trying to get sympathy from the jury."

Salinger didn't take his eyes of Pax. "Your passport lists you as the twin brother of the defendant, Maal Johnson, but now you claim that, in fact, you are not his brother, but his cousin. Is that correct?"

"That's correct," Pax said, in his language. I was standing beside him and translated.

"But why does your passport and the defendant's passport claim you are twin brothers?"

"*The passports were made false*," Pax said.

"The passports were falsified," I translated.

"*Falsified?*" Salinger looked shocked.

"Objection," the young female lawyer called, out of her seat again. "Your honor, my client's passport lists his real mother and father." She pointed down at Pax. "This young gentleman is the only one in this courtroom with a falsified passport."

"*They are both false*," Pax said, grunting, his body twisting in pain.

I reached out and touched his arm. "Pax—"

Salinger raised his voice, spoke sternly. "Ms. LaVenya, could you please translate what the young gentleman just said?"

I didn't look up. I had never felt like Salinger and I were not on the same side. "He said both passports are false."

"*False?*" Salinger looked at the jury. "How are they *false?*"

"*According to our passports, we are sixteen,*" Pax said.

I translated this quickly, so Pax could go on.

"*But we are both nineteen years old.*"

I translated again.

"*Nineteen years old,*" Salinger said, glancing again at the jury. "But why would your passports claim you are three years younger than you really are?"

Pax had to get through a spike in pain before he answered. "*So we could go to school.*"

I translated. Salinger didn't miss a beat.

"Let me ask you, is it true that on the night in question, when your cousin had sexual intercourse with little Anna Jenkins—"

"Objection!"

"Sustained."

"—when your cousin had sexual intercourse with fifteen year old Anna Jenkins, is it true that you told Ms. Jenkins that you and the defendant were nineteen?"

Pax nodded.

"And did the defendant argue with you."

Pax shook his head.

"Objection, your honor," the young lawyer cried, sounding annoyed. "My client may have wanted to impress Ms. Jenkins by claiming to be nineteen, but that is not a crime. The fact of the matter is, there is not one shred of evidence beyond this young gentleman's dubious testimony that my client is anything but the age that his passport clearly states: *sixteen*."

"*Yes, there is.*"

I spoke loudly, hopeful. "He says there *is* other evidence." As soon as the words were out of my mouth, though, I looked at Pax and could feel my hope drain away like rain through sand. What evidence could there be?

"Evidence?" Salinger asked, for the first time sounding unsure of himself.

Pax took a deep, painful breath before going on. *"The day before I came to America, Maal's mother gave me two things to bring to him."* He reached into the breast pocket of his jacket.

"It cannot be," Maal said, in his own language, sitting up like a dog ready to charge. *"We searched everywhere."*

"You did not look under the cabinet of guns," Pax said, and pulled out of his pocket a photograph of a woman with two small children on her lap. *"This is a photograph of Maal and his mother and sister."*

"So I had a sister!" Maal shouted. *"It proves nothing!"*

The judge pounded his gavel for silence and scolded Maal for speaking out. I wasn't listening to what he said because I was staring at a corner of the photograph, which looked like it had been dipped in red ink. It was blood, I realized, but could not understand where it had come from.

"Maal's sister would be sixteen if she were alive today," Pax said, and I translated quickly. *"She was born mid-summer. Two months before the date of birth on Maal's passport."*

"He's making this up!" Maal called out, in English. "A photograph proves nothing!"

The judge again hit his gavel and Maal's lawyers whispered to Maal as I translated. "Pax says that Maal's sister would be sixteen, if she were alive, and was born two months before the birth date on Maal's passport."

"Objection, your honor." The young female lawyer stood up. "We apologize for our client's outbursts, but I'm sure you can agree that a photograph proves nothing about the age of Maal's sister."

"But her certificate of birth proves everything," Pax

said.

"*NO!*" Maal shouted, shooting forward in his seat.

I shouted, as well, translating. "He says a birth certificate *is* proof."

"Your honor," the young lawyer said, "we have contacted the records department of the defendant's country of origin. Apparently there had been a fire seven years ago, and all birth records were destroyed."

"*Except for the blue paper copy given to the parents,*" Pax said.

Out of the corner of my eye I saw Maal jump up out of his seat.

I translated quickly. "Pax says that the parents were given a blue paper copy."

Pax lifted his head to look at Maal. "*It is one of your mother's most prized possessions,*" he said, and groaned quietly as he reached back into his breast pocket. From the pocket he slowly pulled out a folded piece of blue paper.

"*You f---!*" Maal screamed, in his own language, jumping over the desk between himself and Pax. His lawyers reached out to restrain him. "*Using my dead sister against me! I will kill you for this!*"

"*Anna is enwaa!*" Pax shouted back, his face squeezed tight with pain. "*She is younger than your sister!*"

"*I don't care how old she is! I don't care how old I am! Anna wanted me! She wanted me!*"

Maal broke free from his lawyers and leapt at Pax, snatching the piece of blue paper just as two court guards grabbed him, the blue paper falling from his hand and floating slowly, like a feather, to the floor. As a third guard reached down to pick it up, I noticed a corner of the paper was smeared with blood. I stared, couldn't understand. Where did the blood from? How did the blood from the leg wound leak through Pax's jacket? I couldn't stop staring at the piece of paper, confused, not understanding how this could have happened, when the guard unfolded the paper and revealed that it was a blank.

"LIAR!" Maal shouted, squirming desperately to shake off the two guards holding him. *"HE LIED! HE HAD NOTHING! NO PROOF!"*

I was watching Maal laugh wildly, like he believed he had won a great victory, when Pax slumped forward, almost falling out of his chair.

THIRTY FIVE

I jumped in front of Pax and desperately held him in place, as if not letting him fall out of the chair would keep him safe.

"*Thank you, Mrs. LaVenya,*" he said, his voice weak. "*I am sorry it was not easy.*"

He lurched with pain. I moved my hand to his side to hold him up and felt the blood, warm and sticky. I flinched, involuntarily pulling my hand back like I had touched a flame. My hand was covered in bright red. I felt faint, did not know where the blood was coming from—it seemed like it was coming right through the bullet proof vest. I shook my head. I felt like my mind, my whole body, was moving in slow motion.

"*The second shot hit my back,*" Pax said, his voice a whisper.

Even when I heard these words, my mind

took a second to understand them. Then I was shouting for help, hysterical, tears bursting from my eyes. I cannot remember what I said. The tears blurred my vision, and the horror that Pax might be dying in my arms overwhelmed me.

"*Please,*" Pax said, reaching out and taking my hand. "*Tell Maal that the second thing his mother gave me was a message. She said to tell him that he was not always unhappy.*"

"*Pax,*" I pleaded, through my tears, "*please save your strength.*"

"*No guilt. No guilt.*"

"*We'll get you out of here,*" I said. "*We'll get you safe.*"

Pax slowly turned his head from side to side. "*Mordean met me downstairs,*" he said. "*He smells like the ocean on a hot day.*"

"*No,*" I pleaded, blinking away the tears.

"*Please,*" he said, a sound in his throat. "*You*

saved me, bringing me up here. I go without falil crushing my heart."

"*Pax—*"

He squeezed my hand. "*Poppy will be proud. Thank you. Thank you,*" he whispered, his eyes closing as he let go of my hand.

THIRTY SIX

That night my dog Binny was deeply concerned for me. He did not understand why I sat at the kitchen table, sobbing as I listened to the tapes Pax had left behind. Binny sat there right beside me, ready to share as much sadness as was in me. I hugged him, crying harder at his kindness. At one point I got up and gave him a dog biscuit, but he refused to eat it. Instead he held the biscuit gently in his mouth and bowed his head and dropped it at my feet.

I now knew, of course, why Pax had asked for the pieces of different colored paper. All he wanted was a piece of blue paper, but he had asked for the other colors in case someone heard us or saw me getting the paper.

Luckily I was still there in the court room

when Maal's lawyers demanded a mistrial because Pax had lied under oath.

"He did not lie!" I shouted, still wiping away tears.

The young woman lawyer stood smirking as she tapped her fingernail against the table in front of her. "Pax claimed he had *two* things from Maal's mother," she said. "What was the second thing?"

"A *message*," I said, understanding now why Pax had wasted a few of his final breaths talking about his cousin. "Pax told me just now, as he was dying, that Maal's mother wanted him to deliver a message to Maal that he wasn't always unhappy."

At that point they came in with a stretcher for Pax's body. I left with the stretcher and did not know what happened in the court room after that.

Detective Patterson stopped by my house that night. No one from work had ever been to my house, but Patterson was sure I would want to know what had happened after I left with Pax's body.

When the request for a mistrial was denied, Maal's lawyers immediately requested a plea bargain. Given the evidence against Maal and his violent outburst in court, however, they were unable to negotiate for less than ten years of jail time for Maal.

This was welcome news.

As was the initial autopsy report.

Patterson had a friend in the coroner's office. The friend told him the second bullet had entered through Pax's back, just missing the bullet proof vest. It had smashed between two of Pax's ribs and had pierced several vital organs. Even if we had rushed Pax to the hospital, they would not have been able to stop the internal bleeding in time. Pax would have been dead, and without his testimony, Maal would have walked free.

I had a feeling Patterson was disappointed that I wasn't more relieved when he told me there was nothing we could have done to save Pax's life.

"I thought you'd want to know," he said, sounding annoyed, "so you wouldn't feel guilty about letting him testify."

I nodded. "He knew he was dying, Frank," I admitted, not really caring if Patterson thought I was crazy. "Pax could smell his own death as soon as he got shot. He knew if he didn't testify then, he would never testify."

Patterson just looked at me. "I wouldn't doubt it," he said, and gave Binny a final pat on the head before giving me one last look. "It's strange what some people know."

EPILOGUE

I called in sick the next day.

I felt sick.

I was glad, of course, that we had gotten a conviction. I was glad that for the next ten years, Maal would not be able to do to the next girl what he had done to Anna.

But ten years did not seem like a long enough time for *falil*. Maal's sin was permanent. The wound he had inflicted on Anna would not go away in the same way the wound my stepfather had inflicted on me would not go away. It made me sick to think that Maal would get out and would be able to terrorize more women. What happened to some men, that they enjoyed hurting women?

And what could I do to stop them?

I took Binny for a long walk in the icy weather, and we ended up at the shore, looking out at Long Island Sound. The sky had been gray all morning, but when we got to the water, a patch of light opened on the choppy waves. And I knew the two things I needed to do.

The first thing was to become a police officer. Pax's courage had inspired me. I needed to do what I could to stop the terror some men inflict on women. I needed to face these men. I needed to stand in their way.

The second thing I needed to do was get Pax's story out there.

Please help me keep it alive.

Edge of the World Books
a library of books on the edge

Have a hard time finding something you actually enjoy reading?

Edge of the World Books is a small but growing library of books for teenagers looking for something a little edgier than they might find in an ordinary library.

Each book in the collection has a trailer you can watch to decide if it might be something for you. Home-made trailers that fans have created for their favorite books.

Want to nominate a book for the library? Want to publish your own story? Want to compete to create the best trailer for your favorite book? Find out how at edgeoftheworldbooks.com.